THE
COMEBACK

Alex O'Brien

James Lorimer & Company Ltd., Publishers
Toronto

James Lorimer & Company Ltd., Publishers acknowledges funding support from
the Ontario Arts Council (OAC), an agency of the Government of Ontario.
We acknowledge the support of the Canada Council for the Arts, which last
year invested $153 million to bring the arts to Canadians throughout the coun-
try. This project has been made possible in part by the Government of Canada
and with the support of Ontario Creates.

Cover design: Gwen North
Cover image: Shutterstock

Library and Archives Canada Cataloguing in Publication

Title: The comeback / Alex O'Brien.

Names: O'Brien, Alex, 1963- author.

Series: Sports stories.

Description: Series statement: Sports stories

Identifiers: Canadiana (print) 20190187492 | Canadiana (ebook) 20190187514
| ISBN 9781459414808 (softcover) | ISBN 9781459414815 (EPUB)

Classification: LCC PS8629.B72 C65 2020 | DDC jC813/.6—dc23

Published by:
James Lorimer &
Company Ltd., Publishers
117 Peter Street, Suite 304
Toronto, ON, Canada
M5V 0M3
www.lorimer.ca

Distributed in Canada by:
Formac Lorimer Books
5502 Atlantic Street
Halifax, NS, Canada
B3H 1G4

Distributed in the US by:
Lerner Publisher Services
1251 Washington Ave. N.
Minneapolis, MN, USA
55401
www.lernerbooks.com

Printed and bound in Canada.
Manufactured by Marquis in Montmagny, Quebec in December 2019.
Job #181202

Contents

1 Missing OUT

Chris snuck into the stands after the puck dropped. He didn't want his former teammates on the Parry Sound Shamrocks — or their parents — to see that he'd come to watch. He pulled down the brim of his baseball cap and pulled up his collar. He took a seat high in the back corner with the opposing team's parents. One hockey mom smiled at him. Chris started shaking. *I can still leave*, he thought. Instead, he turned his head and stared at the rink.

The championship game was off to a fast start. Trent, the captain of the Shamrocks, raced into the corner and checked the Midland Centennials defender into the boards. Trent passed the loose puck into the slot and the Shamrocks winger rang a shot off the post.

The Centennials broke out quickly. Three passes and the centre crossed the Shamrocks blue line. He faked left and skated right. The Shamrocks defender was fooled. The centre sped by and shot between the goalie's legs. The Shamrocks were down a goal.

If only I could help them, thought Chris. He knew he couldn't. He had quit halfway through the season, a couple of months after taking a hard check in the corner. His leg had been twisted and his knee ligament torn.

Chris felt sad watching his former teammates. *I wish I could play more than anything,* he thought. *But I can't, not feeling like this.* His injury had healed. It had healed before he quit the team. There was another problem, one that Chris didn't want to tell anyone about.

Chris's butt was freezing as the puck dropped to start the second period. The Shamrocks skated hard and had many chances. The Centennials goalie seemed unbeatable until Trent skated end to end and lifted a backhander high over the goalie's shoulder. The game was tied.

Chris hurried to the washroom to hide as the period ended. He couldn't face seeing anyone. He didn't want sympathy or disapproval. He hid in one of the stalls. *I can't believe it's come to this,* he thought. A minute after the start of the third period, he went back to his seat.

The pace was intense. The Shamrocks hit the crossbar. The Centennials missed an open net. Trent rushed the puck up the ice and was knocked down. With the teams tied at a goal each, the buzzer rang and the game went into overtime.

Chris's fingers were freezing. He wished he had brought his gloves. *I'm useless sitting up here*, he thought. *I can't help my team . . . former team.* The Centennials parents were cheering loudly. *At least they're not bothering me. Everyone looks so happy — I wish I felt that way.*

A Shamrocks defender blasted a slapshot from the point. The Centennials goalie stretched out his leg at the last second to make the save.

The Centennials broke out of their end on a two-on-one rush. The Shamrocks defender dove to break up the pass.

Trent stole a puck near centre. He sped down the wing and rifled a wrist shot over the goalie's blocker into the net. Without thinking, Chris jumped up to clap for his team. The Centennials parents glared at him like he was a traitor. Chris sat down again.

For the first time in ten years, the Parry Sound Shamrocks had won the Ontario championship.

Chris watched as his former teammates threw off their gloves and helmets and piled on their goalie. His spark of pride and joy was gone. *I missed it*, he thought. *I missed everything.* The heavy weight he'd been carrying for months came down on him again.

This sinking feeling had started long before his injury. It had grown each week, even more after he was injured. Chris lost all his energy and interest in his favourite things, like hockey, board games and even pizza. He felt guilty for letting down his team and hopeless about the future. The thought of putting skates on again was more than he could bear. He decided to quit rather than return to the team, even though his knee had healed. *There's no way I can play feeling like this,* he had thought.

Lost in worry, Chris forgot that he wanted to be the first to leave the stands. *Now I'll have to wait till my teammates are gone,* he thought. He sat watching the Zamboni flood the ice. When his butt got too cold on the seat, he walked to the top railing and stood there. The stands began to fill as the next game started. Chris watched two house-league teams battle it out for a period. He then made his way through the crowd and down the stairs.

Chris hurried through the lobby towards the exit. Just when he thought he was safe, he bumped into Trent. Some of the French fries Trent had been eating went flying.

"Geez, Chris, watch where you're going," said Trent. "This is my dinner."

"I thought you'd be gone by now," said Chris.

"I stayed to watch my brother's game," said Trent. "Saw the championship, did ya?"

"Yeah, I —"

"Why didn't you drop into the dressing room and wish us luck?" Trent interrupted.

"Oh, I didn't want to jinx you guys."

Trent frowned. "That's stupid. You should've supported us."

"Yeah, I guess you're right. Congrats. The team played great."

"Yeah, we did, didn't we," said Trent. "No thanks to you."

Chris shrugged and headed to the door. *Maybe the guy's right*, thought Chris. *I let everyone down.*

2 Brave FACE

His phone alarm went off. Chris strained to lift his arm to hit snooze. *I don't have the energy to get out of bed*, he thought. *Let alone deal with school.* He pulled the duvet over his head and tried to get back to sleep. The alarm rang a second time and Chris struggled to hit snooze again. *Why can I barely move my arms and legs?*

Chris's mom banged on his bedroom door. "Time to get up, Sunshine!"

"Mom, I told you not to call me that," he said groggily.

"There's a beautiful new day out there just waiting for you," she replied.

Chris ignored her. He wished he could stay in bed for a week. High school was much more work than middle school. There was more homework. The tests were harder. There were more kids. He was tired of pretending to be his old cheerful self. And talking to everyone. It was exhausting.

Chris had no strength to shower or comb his wild blond hair. He pulled on a black Nirvana T-shirt and jeans and shuffled downstairs for breakfast.

"Didn't you wear that shirt yesterday?" asked his mom.

"Yeah, maybe," said Chris. "Who cares?"

"Head back upstairs and put on a clean one — you'll feel much better."

Chris laboured to take off his shirt. His arms felt too heavy to lift. He fought to get the clean shirt over his head. Back downstairs, he picked at the bacon and eggs his mom had cooked for him. He wasn't hungry and left half the food on his plate.

"Have a great day, Sunshine — oops, I didn't mean to call you that," said his mom.

Shaking his head, Chris struggled to put on his coat and boots. He headed up the lane to catch the bus. *I'm never going to make it*, he thought.

The day didn't get any easier once Chris got to school. He sat in the middle row during People and Politics. Ms. Mitchell was teaching them about government. Once, Chris had found the subject fascinating. Today he sat staring down at his desk. *I hope no one can tell that I want to cry*, he thought.

Wait, is Ms. Mitchell talking to me? She called his name, clearly not for the first time.

"I'm sorry, I didn't hear you," said Chris. "I was reading my notes."

"You should have done that last night. Right now, you should be listening to me," she said, smiling.

Chris put on a brave face and did his best to smile back. *I know I should be happy*, he thought. *I've always loved People and Politics. I love Ms. Mitchell's classes. Man, I used to love everything.*

Chris felt horrible. After class, fearing he might break down and show his true face, he rushed out with his head down.

Chris's best friend, Keiko, found him down the hall. He was hunched over and breathing slowly.

"What's the matter, Chris?" Keiko asked.

"Nothing, just tired," he said.

"Are you sure? You don't seem yourself."

"I've had a rough morning."

"It's not just this morning," Keiko said. "You haven't been yourself for a while."

Chris looked up. "What do you mean?"

"Well, I've noticed that at lunch, you barely touch your food. Even when they serve pizza. And sometimes when I tell you something, you don't hear. It's like you're in another world. And you used to comb your hair till you got just the right flow. You don't do that anymore. You don't even comb your hair."

Chris was silent. He had kept his illness hidden from everyone except his parents. He didn't want anyone else to know, especially other kids. *I don't want them thinking I'm crazy*, he said to himself.

"Chris, we're best friends," said Keiko. "What's going on?"

Chris stared into Keiko's pleading brown eyes. He couldn't pretend anymore. "Keiko, I have depression. It's not just feeling a little blue now and then. I get really, really down."

"Oh no . . . I knew something was wrong," said Keiko. "But I had no idea you were depressed." She took Chris's hand. "I feel so bad for you. My aunt had depression. She couldn't get out of bed for days and used to see a psychologist. Are you seeing anyone like that?"

"Yeah, I've been seeing a psychologist for months."

"Is it helping?"

"Yeah, I've made progress," said Chris. "She says I'm too negative. That I blame myself for everything. She's trying to teach me to think more rationally and to use positive self-talk. And she wants me to get back into sports. She says that sports can improve your mood. That physical activity can affect your brain chemicals like anti–depressant medicine. But there's no way I can play again. I've got no energy and the hockey season's over anyway."

"You know, I think she's right," said Keiko. "I feel great after gymnastics. And you don't have to play hockey. You could play soccer. My brother Reo plays every spring and summer. It's early in the season and his team is looking for players."

Chris felt his face grow tense. "No, no, there's no way. I played when I was younger and I wasn't that good. Besides, it's all I can do to get up and get on the bus in the morning. I don't want to cost my parents a fortune and ruin their summer."

"Soccer doesn't cost as much as hockey," said Keiko. "All you need are cleats and shin guards."

Chris shook his head, thinking of Trent scolding him for quitting. "No. I would hate to let another team down," he said. "I can't do it."

"Chris, just think about it. Please?" said Keiko.

The two friends headed to their next class.

★ ★ ★

That night, Chris couldn't get to sleep. His mind was racing. He thought of Trent saying he had abandoned the team. *Why wasn't I there for my team? Why didn't I listen in class? Why can't I hide things better? Keiko must think I'm a wimp.* Chris fought to put these thoughts out of his head. After an hour of worrying, he finally fell asleep.

An hour later, he woke up. He lay in bed staring at the ceiling, unable to sleep. It wasn't like he was just tired. He was exhausted. His stomach felt heavy, his mind cloudy and his heart empty of hope. It took him another hour to doze off.

He woke up again an hour after that. For two long hours, he tossed and turned. *I've got to do something*, he thought. *Something to keep me busy, to concentrate on.*

Brave Face

To be a part of. Even if every muscle in my body resists.
Chris looked at his phone. It was four in the morning.
Tomorrow, I'm signing up for soccer.

3 BALL TIME

Chris's dad drove him to his first soccer practice. When the car stopped, Chris didn't want to get out. He sat staring out the window.

"Everything all right, Chris?" asked his dad. "We're here."

Everything isn't all right, thought Chris. *Why did I sign up? Now I've got a practice and a game every week.* Chris wanted to tell his dad to take him home. *No, I've got to give this a try*, he told himself. *It'll help. My psychologist said so.*

Getting no response, his dad asked, "Aren't you happy to be playing again?"

"I don't know if I'll remember how," said Chris.

"Oh, it'll come back. It's like riding a bike."

"We'll see." Chris shrugged and forced a smile.

He got out of the car and walked to the field. There were many faces he didn't know. It wasn't the crowd he had played hockey with. He sat at the side of the pitch and put on his cleats.

Ball Time

Within seconds, Keiko's brother Reo sat beside him. Reo was one year younger than Chris and Keiko, and much shorter. Chris had often seen him when he and Keiko would hang at her house.

"Hey, Chris, welcome to the Hotspurs," Reo said with a big smile.

Chris didn't think he'd ever seen Reo not smiling. "Hey, good to see ya," he said.

"No, good to see you," said Reo. "Coach Dave will be glad. We needed a player. Now we can sub. Have you met anyone?"

"No, I just got here. There seem to be a lot of newcomers to Canada here."

"Yeah — isn't it great?" said Reo. "Kids from all over the world play soccer. It's cheaper to sign up for than hockey and you don't have to know how to skate."

Cleats on, Chris and Reo took to the field and started passing the ball back and forth. After a few kicks, another teammate wearing the Hotspurs red jersey joined in.

"Farid, this is Chris," said Reo to the player. "Chris is gonna be playing with us. Be gentle with him, he's —"

"Whoa, where are you going with this, Reo?" asked Chris. Chris was worried that Reo was about to tell Farid about his depression. *I bet Keiko told him*, he thought.

"Uh, I was just going to tell him to be gentle with you because you're a hockey player, not a soccer player," laughed Reo.

Farid turned to Chris and smiled widely. "Don't worry, I won't hold it against you," he said. "I learned to skate this past winter and I'm gonna try playing hockey next season. It should be good for a laugh."

"Farid moved here last spring from Syria," said Reo. "He's one heck of a fullback."

"I don't know about that," said Farid. "But I love the beautiful game."

Coach Dave blew his whistle and the team hustled over for the warm-up. Standing along the sideline, Chris saw a late Hotspur running across the pitch. The kid looked familiar. When he got close, Chris saw it was Trent. His heart sank.

Trent squeezed in next to Chris. "Didn't expect to see you here, Chris," he said. "Shouldn't you be home resting your knee?"

"It's better," said Chris. "It's been better for a while."

"So you could have come back and helped out the team?" asked Trent.

"You didn't need help," said Chris. "You won the championship."

Trent gave him a look. "Yeah, but it wasn't easy playing with a short bench because of you."

Luca, the tall team captain, led the warm-up. The

line of players skipped cross-field swinging their arms. They came back the other way skipping and twisting their torsos. Then they jogged out lifting their knees. They came back stretching their groins.

Chris was tired and sore already. He hunched over on the sideline, out of breath and holding his gut. *How am I going to do this every week?* he wondered. The months he spent healing from his injury had left him out of shape.

Trent laughed at him. "Too hard for you, Chrissie Boy? Are you gonna quit this team, too?"

Chris shrugged off Trent's words. He was glad his knee was holding up. *I've just got to prove myself,* he thought.

Coach Dave set up the first drill, a dribbling relay race. He placed four pylons in a zigzag pattern. Then he placed another four in the same pattern. He had the team form two lines of six players at each set of pylons. One at a time, the players were to dribble through their four pylons and back. Then the next player would start. The first squad to go through all their players would win.

Luca led one squad, Trent the other. Chris and Reo ended up with Luca, along with Ethan, Finn and Nick. Farid, Noah, Quinn, Jake and Noodin all lined up behind Trent.

Coach Dave blew the whistle, and Luca and Trent moved their balls around the pylons with skill. It looked to Chris as if the balls were attached to their feet. Luca made it back first by a couple of steps.

Ethan and Noah were off. They weren't as fast, but they kept control. They returned at the same time.

The third and forth dribblers for Trent's squad — Quinn and Noodin — were slower than Nick and Finn. They took the turns wider. They looked like they might lose control of the ball.

Next in line was Chris. Finn passed him the ball with a big lead.

Chris hadn't dribbled in five years. He hit the ball too hard. He had to run to catch up. At the first pylon, he lost control and the ball went the wrong way. He had to bring it back and go around properly. Scared to lose control again, he went around the second pylon so slowly that Farid caught up with him. Chris tried to speed up for the third pylon and the ball rolled away. By the time he reached the final pylon, Farid was already done.

Trent laughed as Chris returned and passed Reo the ball. "Dribble much, Chrissie Boy?" he taunted. "I didn't think you were ever gonna make it back."

"That's enough, Trent," said Coach Dave. He turned to Chris. "Don't worry, we're gonna work on dribbling today. The more touches, the easier it'll get. You'll see."

With a huge lead, Trent's last dribbler, Jake, won the race. There was no way Reo could catch up.

Chris apologized to Luca and his squad for losing the lead. Before anyone could say anything, Farid said, "I want to thank you, Chris."

"For what?" Chris asked.

"Letting me win. I never get the chance," Farid said. Everyone laughed.

The coach ran the team through three more dribbling drills before holding a short scrimmage.

Coach was right, Chris thought afterwards. *With every touch of the ball, I feel more comfortable. I'm getting better. I just have to keep trying.* Chris knew he wasn't going to dribble like Messi, the great Argentine forward, anytime soon. But it was a start.

Reo sat next to Chris as the boys took off their cleats. "Is it working?"

Chris looked up. "What?"

Reo spoke softly. "Did playing soccer make you feel better?"

"So Keiko did tell you?" said Chris.

"Yeah, she thought I could help if I knew," said Reo. "Don't worry, I won't tell anyone."

"Thanks. You had me worried earlier." Chris sized up his new friend. *I can trust this guy*, he thought. "I haven't noticed any big change yet. The nice thing is, I didn't worry all practice. I was too busy trying to get better."

"You'll get better before you know it," said Reo. "Don't let Trent bother you. All he thinks about is winning."

"I know. He was the same with the hockey team," said Chris. "He doesn't realize that I want to win, too."

4 Hard LESSONS

Chris's body was so tired after practice that he had less trouble sleeping that night. Three days later, he was playing his first game. He was nervous, but it wasn't the dread he felt at doing other things. Even things like going to school. He put on his cleats to kick the ball around with Reo and Farid. Seeing Keiko sitting in the stands, he smiled and waved at her. *She really wanted to come see me*, he thought. *I hope I play well.*

Reo passed Chris the ball. "Coach Dave loves triangles," he said. "Make one with us and keep it going as we run and pass. Coach Dave says it's a great way to give support."

Chris joined in and the trio ran together, passing the ball to each other. The triangle changed size and shape as the boys moved among their teammates. Farid sent Chris a lead pass — Chris had to run fast with his head down to get it. Chris's shoulder bumped Trent's shoulder, knocking Trent off his ball.

"Still out of control, are we?" said Trent. "Keep

your distance when the game's on."

"Or better yet, Chris, keep your head up," said Farid. "It'll take a while to get used to. But it'll help you see the field and make better plays."

Man, I should know that from hockey, thought Chris.

Luca led the team through the cross-field warm-up. In the few days since the practice, the aches in Chris's muscles had faded. This time he found the stretches a little easier. *Maybe I* can *handle this*, he thought.

The referee called the captains to centre for the coin toss. Luca lost and the Barracudas captain in his gold jersey chose his end. This meant the Hotspurs would take the opening kickoff.

Coach Dave gathered his players. "Today, I want you to play as a team. Provide support for the ball carrier and talk to each other. Call for that ball if you're in the clear."

The team huddled with their arms over each other's shoulders. "One! One! One for all! Move! Move! Move that ball! Challenge, Hotspurs!"

Eleven Hotspurs and eleven Barracudas took their positions on the pitch. Chris was at right forward. Luca, the leader, was at centre. Trent was at left forward, a fearless striker. Fast-footed Reo was at centre midfield, with Ethan on his left and Noah on his right. Farid held the line on fullback, assisted by Quinn, Finn and Noodin. And Jake was in goal. Nick would serve as the spare.

Chris's heart was beating fast. He had to hold back from crossing centre before Luca touched the ball. Luca tapped it forward. Trent moved to the ball and passed it back to Reo. Thinking of the coach's talk, Chris ran to open space. Reo sent him a long pass. Chris tried to trap or control the ball with his chest. He didn't lean back to cushion the ball, and it bounced to a Barracuda.

"Pass it right to them, why don't you," sneered Trent.

Chris ignored the insult, resolving to do better next time. When a high pass came his way, he leaned back to cushion the ball and it dropped to his feet. Keeping his head up, Chris dribbled up the right side. He saw Luca in the clear ahead and passed the ball to him. Chris kept running. Luca dribbled a couple of yards and passed it back to Chris in a classic give and go. Chris was in scoring range, so he kicked the ball hard. *That didn't feel right*, he thought, as the ball veered off wildly and missed the net. His toes stung. *How could I be so stupid?* Chris thought. *You're supposed to kick using the top of your foot. On your laces, never your toes.*

"What the heck was that?" shouted Trent. "Chris, you're supposed to hit the net."

With minutes left in the first half, the Hotspurs attacked. Luca dribbled up the field and Chris ran to keep up. There were only two Barracudas defenders blocking their way. *Luca wants to pass*, thought Chris. He ran between and past the two defenders before Luca sent the ball forward. The referee's whistle blew and the play was called offside.

Luca told Chris, "You have to wait for my foot to touch the ball before you run past the last defender. Otherwise you put yourself offside."

Trent shook his head at Chris in disgust. "Don't you know anything?"

"You've gotta time your run just right," said Reo. "There's an art to it."

Oh, right, there's offside in soccer, like hockey, Chris thought. *But it's a floating line, not a fixed one like the blue line.* He glanced at Keiko in the stands. She smiled and waved, but Chris felt embarrassed at making such a rookie mistake. He remembered what his psychologist told him about self-talk. *It's okay,* he told himself, *it's coming back. I've been distracted for so long. Now with every play I'm focusing better.*

The second half of the game was a battle. The two teams were evenly matched. One Barracudas striker headed the ball with his forehead off the post. Minutes later, the Barracudas keeper made a beautiful diving save on a hard kick from Trent.

With five minutes left, the Barracudas centre striker faked right and pushed the ball left. He broke free of Farid and dribbled into scoring territory. Farid grabbed his shirt to slow him down. The referee called the foul, flashing a yellow card. The Barracudas were given a free kick.

The Barracudas striker took three steps behind the ball. Farid, Quinn and Nick formed a wall ten yards away to block the kick. Chris should have been the fourth player in the wall, but he forgot to move into place to complete it. Luca yelled to remind him. It was too late.

The Barracudas striker kicked the ball, curving it around the wall and into the net. It was an amazing shot. The Barracudas were up by one.

"I hope you're proud of yourself," Trent told Chris. "You cost us a goal."

"It's not Chris's fault," said Farid. "Coach Dave worked on walls before he joined the team."

"He should have known anyway," said Trent. "He's played soccer before."

Chris felt bad. *I've got to make up for this*, he thought. He fought to get into the open on a free throw. There was only one minute left. From the touch line, Reo threw the ball with both hands over his head to Chris. Chris trapped the ball and looked up. There were Barracudas defenders everywhere. Somehow Chris saw a clear line and passed the ball through three players onto Luca's foot. Luca tapped the ball into the open net. The game ended in a tie.

"Nice pass, Chris," said Luca. "You've got great vision."

Farid ran in and high-fived his new friend. "Nice one, bud. Way to work."

5 Back DOWN

Chris was tired. He sat on the grass by his soccer bag and gulped some water. He took off his cleats and rubbed his sore feet. *I can't believe I dribbled with my head down*, he thought. *I blew a trap, kicked with my toe, went offside. Worst of all, I forgot to join the wall and cost us a goal.*

Stop! Chris told himself. *Stop! None of that matters. What matters is that I learned from those mistakes. I started dribbling with my head up, like I stickhandle in hockey. I leaned back to cushion the ball when I trapped. I remembered that you should kick with your laces, not your toes. And I remembered the offside rule and learned to form a wall on free kicks.*

As Reo joined Chris on the grass, Keiko came over, too.

"Awesome pass, Chris," said Keiko. "You saved the game."

"I've got a lot to learn still," said Chris. "And I couldn't have made that pass without Reo's great throw-in. Thanks, man."

"All in a day's work," said Reo.

Chris laughed at Reo pretending to be humble.

"Chris! It's so great to hear you laugh!" said Keiko.

Chris was still smiling as the trio got up and headed to the parking lot to catch their rides.

That afternoon, Chris met Doctor Bhatt for his weekly therapy session. Chris sat in a cozy brown leather chair beside her. Early on he'd felt embarrassed to be seeing a psychologist. Now he found her easy to talk to. She had a soothing voice and he always felt better after talking with her. He loved her office with its pine furniture and shelves filled with books.

"So, how are things?" asked Doctor Bhatt.

"Not too bad," said Chris. "I played my first game with the Hotspurs."

"Did you have fun?" she said.

That's not a simple question, thought Chris. After a bit, he said, "Yeah. You know what? I did. I made a lot of mistakes, though."

"What kinds of mistakes?" she asked.

"Oh, stupid mistakes. I forgot a lot of things," he said. "But I corrected most of them. And I set up the tying goal."

"Well done," said Doctor Bhatt. "I'm pleased you didn't keep blaming yourself. You're starting to replace negative thoughts with positive ones. That's great. Have you made any friends on the team?"

"Yeah, a couple," said Chris. "There's Reo, my best friend's brother. And this kid from Syria, Farid.

He's funny and nice. The bad news is Trent's on the team, the guy from hockey. He's still giving me a hard time because I quit the Shamrocks."

"And how do you feel about that?" she asked.

"I don't like it, but I try not to let it bother me," said Chris. "He thinks I'm gonna bring the team down. I want to prove I won't."

"That's a good attitude," said Doctor Bhatt. "If his comments get to be too insulting, tell the coach. You don't have to put up with bullies."

"I know. I think I can handle him," said Chris.

Doctor Bhatt smiled. "How's your concentration? Are you able to focus?"

"It's getting better when I play," said Chris. "Having something to learn and do really helps. But it's still not so good at school."

"It should improve soon — cognitive therapy takes time," said Doctor Bhatt. "And it'll take time for your playing soccer to have lasting effects. You've only been playing for a week."

"All I know is I like doing it," said Chris.

"That's a good sign," she said.

"When I'm playing, I don't worry about anything," said Chris. "Except what I'm doing. And I've been using your self-talk. It's not as crazy as I thought — it seems to help."

Doctor Bhatt smiled and they talked a little longer. *Psychologists have more questions than answers,* thought

The Comeback

Chris. *That's okay. It feels good to get things off my chest.* When the session was over, Chris left feeling hopeful.

That evening, Chris's mom made spaghetti and meatballs, his favourite after pizza. His mom told him she was happy his therapy was going well. His dad was pleased that Chris was enjoying soccer. After dinner, they all watched a superhero movie.

Everything was fine till Chris went upstairs to do his homework.

Unable to focus on math, Chris thought about his next game. He remembered all the mistakes he'd made. On the pitch, he'd worked to correct his errors. Here in his room, somehow the future seemed dark. Out of nowhere, negative thoughts rushed into his head. *How could I be so stupid? I almost cost us the game. The team must hate me. I'm useless. I'm gonna cost us the next one.* Chris fought to clear the thoughts. *Stop*, he told himself. *Stop.* But they just kept coming back. Only hours earlier he'd been fine. Now he felt overwhelmed. Like he was drowning. He set aside his math book and crashed on his bed.

Lying in bed, it got worse. Chris felt bad about feeling bad again. *What am I doing?* he thought. *I must be crazy to worry like this all the time. I must be crazy to be seeing a shrink. How am I ever gonna break out of this? I should be happy. Why can't I just be happy?* He lay awake for an hour, his body numb and his mind racing, before he finally fell asleep.

6 Mind FOG

In the morning, Chris silenced his alarm. He had tossed and turned all night, waking up several times. He didn't want to get out of bed. He was exhausted.

His mom knocked on his door. "Wakey, wakey. Rise and shine," she said in a high voice.

"Yeah, yeah, I'm awake," said Chris. "I'll be down in a minute." He sat up and rubbed his eyes. He felt terrible and had no energy. He decided that going to school would be pointless. He would stay home and sleep all day. To do that, he was going to have to fool his mom. He struggled to put on a clean shirt and pants to impress her. He even combed his hair. He headed downstairs to the kitchen table.

"You're looking nice," she said. "All ready to greet the new day."

"Zip-a-dee-doo-dah, zip-a-dee-ay," sang Chris. He remembered his mom singing that song to him when he was little.

His mom laughed.

Chris ate the avocado toast his mom had made for him. His dad had left for work ages ago. Chris usually left for school before his mom went to work, but today he lingered.

"I've got to go," she said. "Can't keep those patients waiting. You'd better hurry or you'll be late."

"I just have to grab my math homework and I'll be gone, too," said Chris.

He went to the window and watched his mom drive down the lane. He shuffled upstairs and fell into bed. He didn't bother to take off his clothes. He was too beat from pretending to be a happy, good kid.

Chris wasn't proud of tricking his mom. *Along with Dad, she's my greatest supporter*, he thought. He liked doing things to please her, but there was just no way he could face the world.

Chris closed his eyes. It took him an hour to fall asleep. Then he slept for eight hours, the sleep like a heavy weight on top of him. When he woke up, he didn't feel rested. His mom would be home soon and he needed to prepare for his game. *Why am I still exhausted?* he wondered. *I've slept all day. What kind of loser sleeps all day?* Chris couldn't keep up the pretence that he was okay if he didn't play soccer.

★ ★ ★

I don't understand, thought Chris when he got to the

soccer field. *I got away with skipping school, but I still feel awful. Like there's a weight crushing my chest.* He forced a smile. He passed the ball with Reo and Farid and ran the warm-up. He knew the routine — he just didn't have any energy.

The Hotspurs were playing the Titans. The orange jerseys the Titans wore made them look bigger than they were. "These guys have a midfielder who controls the field," said Reo. "His name's Amare. He sets up plays like a quarterback."

Chris wasn't listening. He felt numb and stared into space.

"You okay, Chris?" asked Reo.

"What was that?" said Chris.

"I was saying that the Titans have a great midfielder. He can control a game," said Reo.

"I see," said Chris.

The match began. The Titans passed the ball back to Amare. With one touch, he received it and scanned the field. A Titans player was running down the sideline. That player was Chris's man to tag. It was Chris's job to make sure he didn't get the ball. The Titans attacker slowed down. Chris slowed down with him. When the attacker raced ahead, Chris was caught off guard. Amare sent the attacker a long lead pass. The Titans player ran to the ball and dribbled towards the net. He kicked the ball into the corner.

Trent was fuming. "That was your man, Chris," he

scolded. "Don't let him get away like that."

Chris wanted to say he was sorry. To tell Trent that his legs felt like they were made of lead. He couldn't find the strength to speak.

"Don't worry, Chris," said Farid. "Just watch for changes of speed."

Midway through the first half, Chris retrieved a loose ball. He dribbled up the field. Two Titans defenders stood between Chris and the goal.

Reo ran over to provide support. "Chris, Chris, I'm open!" he shouted. "I'm open! I'm open!"

Chris dribbled straight into the defenders. One stole the ball from him.

"I was open," Reo told Chris. "Didn't you hear me calling?"

"No," said Chris.

"But I was shouting," said Reo.

Chris shrugged and walked away. His head felt heavy. It was like his ears were plugged. Nothing could reach him.

Chris's playing was no better in the second half.

He missed a pass from Noah that he could have got if he'd run to the ball.

He was too slow to provide support to his teammates.

Coach Dave yelled for Chris to pass the ball wide. Trent was in the clear on the other side. Chris didn't hear and lost the ball to Amare. Amare chipped the ball deep into the Hotspurs end. The Titans striker headed it into the net.

"What is wrong with you?" Trent yelled at Chris. "You can't do anything right!"

"I don't know," Chris mumbled.

"That's all you've got to say?" said Trent. "After costing us two goals? And the game!"

"Take it easy, Trent," said Farid. "Everyone has a bad game now and then."

"I haven't seen him play a good one yet," said Trent.

Chris wished the game was over. He wanted to be back home in bed. *Why did I sign up for this torture?* he wondered.

After the final whistle blew, Chris rushed to take off his cleats. He didn't want to talk to anyone. Reo and Farid tried to cheer him up. Chris just nodded and got up to leave.

Coach Dave nabbed Chris before he could escape. "Chris, could you gather up the flags and balls? Take them over to the shed. And pick up any water bottles lying around. It's our turn to clean up."

By the time Chris was done, everyone was gone except for Coach Dave.

"Is everything all right, Chris?" asked the coach. "You weren't yourself today."

Chris felt like his whole world was crashing down. He fought to hold back tears. "Yeah, all's good," he said. "I just had an off game."

"Are you sure?" said the coach. "You look kind of down. No problems at school or home?"

Chris couldn't hold back any longer. He burst into tears. "Nothing like that," he said between sobs.

"What's the matter, Chris?" said Coach Dave. "Maybe I can help?"

"I . . . I have depression," said Chris. He wiped his eyes with his sleeve. "It started last year out of nowhere. It got worse when I injured my knee. I'm in therapy. I thought I was getting better. I don't know why I felt so bad today. And played so bad. It's like my mind was trapped in fog."

"You didn't play that badly," said Coach Dave. "You're still learning and you weren't yourself. I'm impressed you even tried. I can only imagine how hard it would be to play feeling as you do. You know, maybe it would be easier if you told the team. Sometimes the facts go a long way towards fighting fear, ignorance and misunderstanding. What do you think?"

"I don't know. What if they think I'm crazy?" said Chris.

"I don't think they'll think that," said the coach. "But if they do, we can work together to set them straight."

Chris wasn't sure. *No matter how well they take it, it will be embarrassing*, he thought. But it felt good to tell the coach. It might feel good to tell his teammates, too. "I guess I'll give it a try," he said. "I sure don't want to ever play as bad as I did today."

Mind Fog

"Great, we'll do it at the start of next practice," said Coach Dave. "I find people can be more understanding when they know the truth."

Chris pulled a sweaty towel out of his soccer bag and wiped his nose.

7 CURVEBALL

Chris arrived for practice feeling anxious. He'd never talked to a large group like this. And he'd never told other kids his problems. *What if they think I'm nuts?* he thought. *What if they don't want me around?*

After stretches, Coach Dave called everyone over. "Chris has something important to say. Listen closely and remember that we're all in this together. Chris, you have the floor."

Chris stood before the Hotspurs. He didn't know where to begin. No words would come. Then he said, "Uh, guys, I have depression. I get really sad for no reason. Not the usual sadness you get from flunking a test or losing a game. A heavy feeling that weighs down every part of my body. At times, it's like there's nothing good in the entire world. And I'm not in control of it — it's in control of me. But I'm getting help and improving. Playing soccer really helps."

"Thanks for sharing that, Chris," said Coach Dave. "The more we know, the more we can help." The coach smiled and walked to Chris's side. "Does anyone have any questions? I'll start: How's depression different from just being sad?"

"It lasts longer. Something bad doesn't have to happen for you to feel it. And it's deeper — it affects everything," said Chris.

Chris looked to his teammates. No one had their hands up. Then Jake, the keeper, blurted out, "I thought only girls get depressed."

"No, boys do, too," said Chris. "My doctor told me boys just don't like to talk about it. But you have to talk about it to get better."

Reo stood up. "Do you have to take any drugs? My aunt had to take them. My uncle called them her happy pills."

"I don't take any drugs," said Chris. "It's an option, though. My doctor's using cognitive therapy and sports therapy. Playing sports can help . . . sports affects our brain chemicals like drugs do."

Trent raised his hand.

Oh no, what's he going to ask? thought Chris.

"Isn't depression a sign of weakness?" said Trent. "And isn't it all just in your head?"

"No, no, those are myths," said Chris. "Depression can happen to anyone: boxers, athletes, even world leaders. It's just like other ways of being sick, only it involves brain chemicals. It can be serious."

"That may be," said Trent. "But can you play

soccer? This team wants to win. We can't be babysitting you. What if you start crying in the middle of a game or have no energy? We don't need that."

"I want to win, too," said Chris. "I'm getting better. I think I can play well if given the chance."

"I don't —" began Trent.

Luca, the captain, interrupted. "I think Chris can play well, too. I've seen what he can do on the field. He has good vision. He's a Hotspur and we should give him a chance. Besides, we need a spare."

"I agree," said Farid. "When I first came to Canada, I wasn't in a good place. I'd seen horrible things back home. My family was lucky to get out, but the refugee camps were brutal. And when I got here, I had no friends and didn't know anything about the country. I was afraid. I felt sad and alone. The doctor said I had anxiety, maybe even post-traumatic stress disorder. Talking to a psychologist really helped. So did talking to my family and friends. Slowly I got better. Chris deserves a chance to get better, too."

"I agree," said Noodin.

That was the first time Chris had heard Noodin speak. Then, one by one, everyone except Trent voiced their support for Chris.

"Well, if that's what the team wants, then okay," said Trent. "But I think we're taking a risk. This is a soccer team, not a therapy group."

Coach Dave thanked Chris for his honesty and the

team gave Chris a loud cheer: "One! One! One for all! Move! Move! Move that ball! Challenge, Hotspurs!"

Feeling better, Chris followed the team onto the field for the drills. Despite Trent's doubts, the rest of the Hotspurs were behind him. Their support gave Chris confidence. He worked hard at the passing and defending drills.

"You looked good out there, bud," said Farid. "How're ya holding up? If you don't mind me asking."

"No worries, I'm chill," said Chris. "It's a relief not having to hide anything. And when I'm playing, I don't think anything . . . sad. I feel almost normal."

"Nice," said Farid.

Chris smiled. "Did you play on a soccer team back in Syria?"

"You bet," said Farid. "Till my family moved into a camp, because of the fighting."

Chris was amazed how cheerful Farid was. *Only a year ago he was living in the middle of a civil war,* he thought. "Do you like it in Canada?" he said.

"I love it," said Farid.

"Even the winter?" asked Reo.

Farid laughed. "I did freeze my butt off! But I learned how to skate."

Coach Dave called the team over to the penalty area in front of the net. "Now we're gonna work on curving the ball," he said. "Like your favourite players. It's a great way to trick the keeper." Coach Dave placed a ball down twelve yards from the goal where penalty kicks were taken. "To curve left, you've got to kick the right side of the ball," he said. "This creates a spin that moves the ball left." The coach moved five steps back from the ball. "So here we go."

Coach Dave took five steps forward and planted his left foot. He kicked the ball on the right side. The ball went to the right where he aimed and then spun back into the top left corner. "Now it's your turn, guys. Half of you practice here. The rest, come with me to the other net. And don't get discouraged. It takes lots of practice."

Chris was impressed. *Coach really knows how to bend a ball*, he thought. He was also worried. He was just getting used to kicking a ball straight. How would he be able to curve it?

Reo was first up. He took a few short steps and kicked the ball smoothly. It went right and then curved slightly into the net. His kick was accurate, but not hard.

Jake shot his ball hard, straight, high and long. "What do you expect from a keeper?" he joked. "I'm used to sending my kicks halfway up the field."

Farid blasted a shot that curved into the top corner. Chris was sure the kick was even harder than Coach Dave's.

Luca took three long strides and kicked a low curveball that just missed the left corner.

"Watch this, boys, and learn," said Trent. He approached the ball with confidence. But something looked different. Trent appeared to kick the left side of the ball, not the right. The ball started left where he'd aimed and then curved right into the corner.

"That's a clockwise spin, boys," said Trent. He pointed to Chris. "Let's see what you've got, Chrissie Boy."

Chris started five steps back. He ran in too fast and planted his foot too soon. He had to reach with his leg and barely hit the ball. The ball dribbled left and didn't reach the net. His leg shot out. Off balance, Chris fell backwards, legs up. Slowly, he stood and dusted off his shorts and jersey.

"What was that?" sneered Trent. "You looked like a lunatic."

Chris turned red. He didn't know what to say.

"Give him time," said Reo. "It was his first try."

"Or what?" said Trent. "He'll have another panic attack?"

"I don't think you know what you're talking about, Trent," said Farid. "Chris is still learning."

"Look, he's a wild card," said Trent. "Who knows, he could have a nervous breakdown."

"That's not right," said Farid.

"I agree, that isn't right," said Coach Dave. The boys hadn't seen him come back from helping at the other net. "Trent, you're going to sit next game. It's wrong to smear a teammate and spread fear. Chris is a good player. He's under proper care. He's given no one any reason to fear anything — period."

"I'm fine with that," said Trent. "As long as the rest of you are fine with losing."

"There are worse things than losing," said Coach Dave. "One is not supporting your teammates."

Chris felt embarrassed. He didn't mean for Trent to get in trouble. Chris just wanted Trent to see that he could help this team.

8 Ball HOG

It was game day: Chris's first after telling the team he had depression. Chris didn't know how he felt about Trent having to sit out the game. But he couldn't let Trent's insults bring him down. *Why dwell on those?* he thought. *I know I'm no lunatic. What's important is proving I can play. That I can pull my weight. That despite my illness, I'm strong.*

The Hotspurs were playing the Strikers.

Chris took his position to Luca's right.

"These guys are awesome passers," the Hotspurs captain said softly, pointing at the Strikers in their green jerseys. "We're gonna have to work hard to keep the ball."

Chris nodded. He was ready to work hard.

Luca tapped the ball forward to Chris. The usual play was for Chris to pass the ball back to a midfielder. That kept the ball safe and gave teammates time to get open. But this time Chris kept the ball to himself. He dribbled up the right side. He faked left and went right.

This got him by the first defender.

Chris was proud. Now everyone would see what he could do. Rather than pass, he kept on dribbling. He made it a few steps and was met by a big Strikers defender. Chris had no time or space. The defender tackled hard and stole the ball.

The Strikers defender passed the ball. Reo could tell where it was going and cut off the pass. He kicked the ball back to Chris.

Chris knew what he should do. Passing was crucial. The soccer field was huge and running with the ball was exhausting. Not like hockey, where the rink was smaller and the skater could glide.

"Move the ball! Move the ball!" shouted Trent from the side of the field.

In his head, Chris knew he should move the ball quickly. He heard the words but they didn't sink in. Instead of passing the ball, he hogged it. He dribbled over centre. For a while he was in the clear. Then he got tired. He slowed down. The Strikers midfielder caught up and stole the ball.

Within seconds, the midfielder passed the ball up the field. The Strikers forward dribbled three steps and kicked it sideways across the pitch. Another Strikers forward raced to the net and headed the ball off the crossbar. It was a beautiful passing play. The Strikers had almost scored.

Chris walked by the Hotspurs sideline area.

Trent was shouting and flailing his arms. Chris heard him complain, "Coach, you've got to do something about Chris. He's killing us. I could go in for him. At least I know how to pass." Coach Dave scowled and motioned for Trent to sit back down.

Trent's opinion doesn't matter, thought Chris. *I'll just try harder.* He had told the team about his depression. His teammates had been great. It was time to show them what he could do.

Chris received a pass in the Strikers corner. Reo was behind him calling for the ball. Luca was in the penalty area shouting for a pass. But Chris was too busy trying to break free of three Strikers to hear. Frustrated, he blasted a shot. One defender right in front of Chris easily blocked the kick. It was a wasted chance.

Reo called to Chris. "Hey, you've got support. I was behind you!"

Chris nodded. "I know. I thought I saw an opening and went for it."

At halftime, Chris sipped his water and ate slices of orange. He saw Trent whispering to the coach, who kept shaking his head "no."

Luca came over to Chris. It looked like he wanted to say something. Luca opened his mouth to speak. Then he closed it and walked away.

A minute later, Farid did the same thing.

What's up with these guys? Chris wondered.

Having done little in the first half, Chris wanted

to try even harder in the second. *These guys have got to learn that depression doesn't make me weak*, he thought. *And Trent's got to see I'm useful.*

He tried fancy foot moves and lost the ball every time.

He tried kicking the ball into open space and running after it. That worked once, but the Strikers caught on and beat him to the ball the other times.

Luca got clear in the attacking zone. He yelled for the ball. "Chris, send it, send it!"

Chris looked up and decided to shoot instead. He was so far from the net, the ball didn't even make it to the goalkeeper.

Time's running out, thought Chris, with only three minutes left. *I've got to do something. We're stuck in our end and I've got to get the ball out.*

Jake yelled, "Reo's open. Use him, Chris, use him!"

Chris ignored the Hotspurs keeper. He knew the best way to advance the ball was to pass. But he didn't do it. Chris dribbled up the middle of the field, right in front of his own net. The Strikers centre challenged hard. Chris tried to put the ball between his opponent's legs. The centre stole the ball, took a step right and blasted a shot into the top corner. The Strikers were up a goal.

The referee placed the ball at centre. The Hotspurs had one minute to tie the game.

Chris watched as Luca passed the ball to Ethan. He felt sad. *If only I had one more chance*, Chris thought.

Ethan passed it back to Farid, who had moved up. Farid sent the ball long to Reo, who was racing in. Reo passed to Luca. Luca blasted a long shot that the keeper dove to save.

The keeper got up with the ball and kicked it. The whistle blew. The Hotspurs had lost.

Chris walked to his bag by the side of the field.

Trent was waiting. "What were you doing out there, you hog? You cost us the game. We had so many missed chances. You just kept giving the ball away. You have to pass in soccer."

Chris felt terrible. "Sorry, man, I don't know what I was doing. I just —"

Trent interrupted. "I don't want to hear your crazy excuses. You're useless."

Coach Dave heard and said, "Trent, you're not being helpful. If you keep it up, you'll be sitting another game. Now hush up and get out of here."

Coach Dave took Chris aside. "Is everything okay, Chris?" he said.

"Yeah, but I couldn't do anything right out there," said Chris. "Why do you ask?"

"It's just that up till now, you've played well," said the coach. "You've made a few beginner mistakes, but you listened and corrected them. And in practice you've shown that you're a good passer. You always see the open player and get the ball to him. Except today. Today I don't think I saw you pass the ball once."

"I must have passed it once," said Chris.

"No, I don't think so," said Coach Dave.

"Wow, why didn't you say something?" asked Chris.

"I know you've been feeling down," said the coach. "I didn't want to make things worse. I thought soon you'd start passing again. You didn't."

"I had no idea," said Chris. "I was just trying to work extra hard to show the team I can help. Coach, whatever you do, don't go easy on me. If I'm doing things wrong, tell me. I want to make the right plays."

Coach Dave wiped his brow. "What a relief," he said. "I wasn't sure if I could ever correct your play again."

"Just treat me like everyone else," said Chris. "I can take it."

"I know you can," said the coach. "Remember, Chris, you don't have to be a superstar. You just have to play your game."

"Okay, Coach," said Chris.

He packed up his bag and headed to the parking lot. *I better tell the others not to go easy on me either,* he thought. *Luca and Farid probably wanted to tell me to pass and were scared to.*

9 High and WIDE

Chris arrived at the pitch looking forward to playing the Tornadoes. *This game, I'm gonna pass*, he thought. *Like before.* At first Trent's insults had hurt him, but Chris had talked himself out of letting them keep him down. *I've learned my lesson*, he thought. *I can't do it all on my own. I've got to pass.*

After warm-up, Reo said, "I don't know how a team in boring grey jerseys can score so many exciting goals."

"The Tornadoes score a lot?" asked Farid.

"Yeah, their strikers can dance," said Reo.

"Well, you can dance, too, Reo," said Chris. "And they haven't run into the Mighty Farid. He's like a brick wall."

"I don't know," laughed Farid. "Sometimes there's a lot of holes in that wall."

The game started. Luca sent the ball over the centre line to Chris. Chris was pleased that he had the captain's trust back. Chris kicked the ball back to Reo.

"Beautiful pass, Chris! Beautiful!" cheered Coach Dave from the sideline.

It wasn't that beautiful, Chris chuckled to himself. *But it was a pass. Coach Dave must have been worried that I'd never pass again.*

The Tornadoes broke up the Hotspurs attack. Their midfielder passed to a striker in the Hotspurs end. The striker dribbled right at Reo. He dropped his left shoulder and pushed the ball right. Reo was left moving the wrong way. The striker ran towards Farid. He spun his foot around the ball. Farid stumbled and looked confused. The striker dribbled by and shot into the lower corner.

The Tornadoes had scored first.

"I can't believe he tricked me with his fancy footwork," said Farid.

"Don't worry. He found the holes in my wall, too," said Reo.

Chris was shocked that the Tornadoes striker had beaten his team's two best defenders. This was going to be a tough one.

The Hotspurs didn't give up. Quinn passed to Reo. Reo dribbled while Chris fought to get open. Reo sent Chris a lead pass that Chris ran to meet. He dribbled down the side. He saw Luca heading towards the goal. Chris timed a perfect cross. His kick sailed to the far post. Luca raced in and headed the ball into the net.

Luca smiled and nodded at Chris. "Looks like you've learned to pass again. Nice work."

Chris could see that it was a friendly jest, not an insult. Before the game, Chris had told Luca and his other teammates not to go easy on his play. He was glad they had listened.

The Tornadoes came back strong. At kickoff, they passed their way up the field. One striker dribbled in. He pushed the ball between Farid and the left defender. He ran to catch up and blasted a kick. Jake dove. The ball burst through his fingers.

"They keep finding new holes in our wall," said Farid.

"I hate to tell you, Farid," said Trent. "Whatever wall you might have had has been knocked down."

The Tornadoes were up two to one.

Chris could see Trent was fired up. So was Chris. Both players challenged hard in the Tornadoes' penalty area. Chris lost the ball to a defender. Trent won the ball back. The defender kicked hard at the ball. He missed and got Trent's ankle. Trent shrieked in pain. Chris was impressed that Trent didn't go down. The referee blew his whistle and gave the Hotspurs a penalty kick.

Trent took three steps back from the ball. He ran in and kicked low and hard. The ball shot into the left corner. The keeper didn't have a chance.

The score was tied at two.

With one minute left in the half, Chris took a pass in scoring range. He was in the clear. The Hotspurs could take the lead. Chris pushed the ball forward. He ran and kicked the right side to curve it left. He got under the ball and it shot up ten feet over the crossbar.

"What was that?" jeered Trent. "A field goal? You just blew our chance to take the lead."

It wasn't a friendly jest, like Luca's. But Chris didn't let Trent's jibe get to him. *I just learned that shot*, he told himself. *I've got to practice more. Maybe ask someone for help.* The whistle blew and Chris walked off the pitch.

Chris sat with Reo eating orange pieces.

"You look like you're having fun out there," said the midfielder.

"I am," said Chris. "I'm pumped."

"Why's that?" asked Reo.

"I don't know. I'm just really into it," said Chris. "When I get playing, I don't seem to worry."

"Well, you're playing better," said Reo. "Coach Dave couldn't be happier with your passing."

Chris laughed. "Yeah, he was scared I'd never pass again."

"I was feeling the same," said Reo. "It's great to have you back."

The Tornadoes started the second half with the ball. The centre tapped it to his right striker. The right striker passed it to the left striker, who was already running. The centre and the right striker raced down the field, crossing paths. The left striker dribbled to the Hotspurs penalty area and crossed the ball. Farid had the right striker covered. The pass went to the open centre. He pounded a shot into the corner.

"These guys are tornadoes all right," said Reo. "They twirl through you, leaving nothing but broken dreams."

"You've got that right," said Jake.

"I don't think we can beat them," said Ethan.

"Me neither," said Finn.

Chris didn't like his teammates feeling down. *Self-talk motivates me*, he thought. *Maybe I can use it to rally the team.* "Don't give up now, guys," he said. "We can do this. We've seen how they play, so we can use that."

The Tornadoes were up by a goal. Their coach moved one striker back into the midfield to defend the lead. The Hotspurs couldn't move the ball through the solid defence.

Even Chris was beginning to wonder if they could win. The Tornadoes kept forcing Farid to kick before he was ready. Stealing Reo's passes. Blocking Trent's shots. With five minutes left, it looked hopeless.

We can't give up, thought Chris. He fought for the ball in the Tornadoes corner. He won the challenge. He passed to Reo and ran, and Reo passed back. Chris scanned the field. He saw Farid charging in. Chris kicked the ball through three defenders. With one touch Farid shot hard. The ball went right and then spun left into the top corner.

"Beautiful, Farid!" said Trent. He turned to Chris. "That's how you're supposed to do it."

The Comeback

Chris shrugged. He knew he had to work on bending the ball. He was just happy that the game was tied.

"What was beautiful," said Luca, "was that pass. Way to thread the needle, bud. You did all the work."

"Well, not quite all of it," joked Farid. "I did kick in that smooth pass."

Chris laughed. "You did, my friend. Now we need another one."

There were two minutes left. The Tornadoes attacked fiercely. Farid was onto their moves and shut down their strikers. He won a challenge and sent the ball up the field. Chris trapped it. He dribbled three steps and saw Trent running towards the defensive line. Chris timed his pass perfectly. He hit the ball just before Trent ran past the defenders. Trent was alone and had the ball. He dribbled in and shot over the goalie's head into the net.

The Hotspurs cheered.

Chris put up his hand to high-five Trent.

Trent sneered and walked away.

I guess the guy doesn't appreciate a good pass, thought Chris. *Oh well, at least I've mastered the offside rule.*

After the game, Coach Dave praised Chris. "You showed character out there today," he said. "You rallied the boys and you never gave up."

Chris left the field feeling proud. Now if only he could learn how to bend that ball . . .

10 Off the BAR

Chris arrived early for the big game. It was the second-last match of the season. Based on their place in the standings, and that of their opponents, the Hotspurs had to win or tie this game and the next to make the playoffs.

Chris joined Reo and Farid kicking a ball.

"So are the Stingers any good?" Chris asked.

"They lost in the semi-finals last year," said Reo. "But this year they picked up a newcomer from Argentina. He's a little Messi. Scores a lot of big goals."

Farid looked concerned. "So we're in trouble?"

"We just have to stop him," said Chris.

"Well, I'm gonna make it my mission to shut this Mini Messi down," said Farid.

He sounds determined, thought Chris. *Maybe I can encourage him.* "You're the guy to do it," he said.

"Did you forget the holes in my wall last game?" Farid teased.

"I'm sure you've patched them up," said Chris.

Luca led the warm-up stretches and a heartier cheer

than usual. "One! One! One for all! Move! Move! Move that ball! Challenge, Hotspurs!" they roared.

Passing by Chris, Trent snarled, "I hope you've taken your happy pill. We can't afford to lose."

"I told you," said Chris. "I'm not on meds."

"Oh, well, maybe you should be," said Trent. "Remember, field goals don't count in soccer."

He doesn't care that I set up his winning goal last game, thought Chris. *All he remembers is one bad shot. I'm not going to let him get to me. This game's too important.*

The Stingers lost the coin toss. The Hotspurs chose their end and the Stingers began on attack.

As the Stingers centre touched the ball, Chris ran to their midfielder. He wanted to catch him off guard. The ball beat Chris there.

The midfielder's first touch was fast. He passed to Mini Messi, who dribbled down the side.

Chris had to hustle to catch up. Running beside his opponent, he tried his first slide tackle. He slid with one leg out and one leg bent in. The idea was to hit the ball away with his foot. He missed and struck Mini Messi's ankle hard.

The Stingers striker shrieked in pain. He fell to the ground scowling and holding his foot. The whistle blew and the referee flashed a yellow card, Chris's first.

"Taking your troubles out on the other team, are you?" said Trent.

"No, trying to stop an attacker," said Chris.

"Well, that was embarrassing," said Trent. "The Hotspurs play fair."

The words stung. Chris prided himself on playing fair. Couldn't Trent see that?

The Stingers midfielder took the direct kick. He sent the ball long to Mini Messi, who had recovered. At the last second, Farid jumped high and headed the ball to safety. If Farid had missed, the striker would have had an open path to the net.

"The wall's back, boys," said Farid. "The wall is back."

"Sometimes I think your head is made of brick," teased Reo.

"Just another brick in the wall," said Chris, thinking of a really old song his dad liked.

"Just another bad joke," groaned Farid.

The two teams traded chances. Mini Messi blasted a long shot. Jake jumped and punched the ball over the crossbar. Luca raced down the wing and drove a shot just wide of the Stingers net.

With one minute left in the half, Chris got the ball in his end. Mini Messi was right on him. Chris dropped his shoulder to feint. Mini Messi wasn't tricked. The striker challenged hard and stole the ball. He dribbled in and beat a surprised Jake.

Chris realized he should not have tried to feint deep in his own end when he was the last man back. It was too dangerous. The Stingers were up by a goal.

The Comeback

Walking off the field, Trent ripped into Chris. "You handed him that one. You may as well have kicked it in yourself."

"I wasn't thinking. My bad," said Chris.

"Wake up out there," said Trent. "You're losing touch with reality."

Another rookie mistake, thought Chris. *But I'm not losing touch with reality — I'm learning.*

Chris poured water over his head. It was hot and he was sweaty. He ate orange slices and listened to Reo describing Mini Messi's sweet plays. The skilled striker seemed to have a hundred moves. Chris nodded but didn't speak. *I've got to get back out there*, he thought. *I've got to make up for my mistake.*

The Stingers came on strong. They controlled the ball for long periods. To Chris, the second half seemed to fly by.

True to his word, Farid shut down Mini Messi. The star striker didn't get another goal after Chris's mess-up. Farid was always there.

Jake picked up a loose ball in the penalty area. He kicked it down the field. With two minutes left, he left the net and joined the attack, but his kick went astray. Mini Messi beat Luca to the rolling ball. The striker faked a kick, pulled the ball back with his foot and moved the other way. Mini Messi braced to blast a long shot into the open Hotspurs net.

Jake raced back to the net. It was a hopeless cause.

As Mini Messi's foot struck, Chris dove in front of the rising ball. The ball bounced off Chris's chest into Luca's feet. Luca dribbled up the field and crossed the ball to Reo. Reo shot a high blaster that hit the crossbar. The ball bounced down and off the keeper's back into the net.

The score was tied.

The Hotspurs were still in the running for a playoff spot.

Reo cheered wildly. Jake wiped the sweat off his brow.

"I've never seen anything quite like that," said Luca. "And I've been playing soccer a long time."

"What a way to score," said Farid.

"What a block," Reo told Chris. "That makes up for earlier."

"Yeah, I got lucky," said Chris.

"We got at least three lucky breaks on that one," added Jake.

"Some days the breaks fall your way," said Luca.

"And some days they don't," said Trent. "Don't celebrate too much. We still have to win or tie the next one."

The two teams lined up to shake hands. As he passed Chris, Mini Messi patted him on the back. "Nice block!" he said. "I thought I had one."

"Thanks. You've got great moves," said Chris.

Mini Messi smiled. "Thanks, man!"

11 Holding STRONG

I thought I'd be more nervous, thought Chris. It was the last regular season game and the Hotspurs couldn't afford to lose. The Ravens, dressed in black, looked big and tough. Chris reminded himself, *I'm with my friends playing a game I love.* Even Keiko had come to watch this one.

"Reo tells me the Ravens play like robots," said Keiko. "They don't sweat and they never get tired."

"Maybe they are robots," said Chris. "Big angry bird robots out to destroy us."

"Now you've got *me* scared," teased Keiko. "More for my life than you guys losing."

"Don't worry," Chris told her. "It's hearts that win games, and robots don't have them."

Chris lined up at centre. Across from him stood a giant Raven. *That kid must be six feet tall*, thought Chris. *And is that a beard? Maybe I should be worried.*

The Ravens started on the attack. They moved the ball quickly. They were always shifting to open space. When in trouble, they switched the attack, kicking to where there were fewer Hotspurs players. The Hotspurs barely touched the ball for ten minutes.

I can't stand around watching these guys, thought Chris. *I've got to challenge harder.* Using his body, Chris angled a striker towards the touchline and fought for the ball. The two battled until the ball bounced off the Ravens player and out of bounds. It was a Hotspurs throw-in.

Hurry, hurry, you can catch them off guard! Chris saw Luca open in scoring range. The captain was far ahead, farther than Chris had ever thrown a ball. Chris ran three steps and planted his feet. Bending his elbows and arching his back, he brought the ball behind his head. He sprung his arms forward as hard as he could, releasing the ball above his head.

The ball flew thirty yards to Luca. Luca settled the ball and drove it by the diving Ravens keeper.

The Hotspurs were up by one.

"That was some throw!" said Luca.

"Yeah, I think we've found your talent," said Farid.

"No kidding!" Reo agreed. He turned to Chris. "You've got to take more throw-ins."

Chris rubbed his shoulder in jest. "I'm not sure my back can handle another one."

"Too bad soccer's mostly played with the feet," said Trent. "Maybe football's your game."

"Come on, Trent," said Luca. "I've never seen you throw a ball that far."

The Ravens regained control quickly. With crisp

passes, they moved the ball into the Hotspurs end. One big angry bird dribbled into the penalty area. Farid got between him and the goal. The forward passed the ball over to a charging midfielder who pounded it into the open corner. The shot was so hard, Chris thought it might break the netting.

The half ended tied at one.

Refreshed after halftime, the two teams took to the field.

"Challenge hard, boys," said Luca. "We can't lose this one."

The Ravens came out strong. They kept control for a long time. Jake made save after save.

Suddenly, a Ravens forward got free of Reo in the corner. The forward had a clear path to the net. Chris raced in. He had to get that ball out of bounds! He thought a slide tackle might work. But the last time he'd tried one, he'd missed. Chris wouldn't let that stop him from trying again. When he got within striking distance, he launched his slide.

Whoosh! Chris felt contact. The ball tumbled out of bounds. It felt good to get that tackle right this time.

The Ravens had a corner kick. A stocky defender lined up at a slight angle to the ball. He drove his foot through hard and sent the ball high out front of the net. The six tallest Ravens charged in. One giant bird leaped into the air above Farid and headed the ball into the net. Jake didn't have a chance.

The Ravens were up by one with two minutes left.

"This is it," said Luca at centre. "Our season is on the line."

A Ravens midfielder intercepted Noah's desperate pass. The midfielder sent a long pass deep into the Hotspurs end.

Jake ran out to catch the ball. The keeper drop kicked the ball sixty yards. It flew into a crowd of Ravens and Hotspurs. The Ravens were taller. *I don't have a chance*, thought Chris. *These guys can outjump Farid.*

Still, Chris hurled himself into the air. To his surprise, his head made contact. He had timed his jump right. The ball flew to Luca's feet as Chris fell down hard. Luca dribbled in and launched a long shot that sailed over the keeper's head into the net. Chris got up and checked his knee. Just a bruise. His teammates cheered and mobbed the captain.

The Hotspurs had tied the game. The point for this tie gave them just enough in total to make the playoffs!

After the game, Coach Dave said, "You guys played great. But why'd you wait so long? You almost gave me a heart attack."

The whole team laughed.

"The semi-final is a week from today," said Coach Dave. "Make sure you eat well and get lots of rest. Oh, and there's gonna be a scout out to see the game. He'll be choosing players to invite to the regional team tryout. That's the team that will represent our region in the Ontario Summer Games. Not that you need the extra pressure."

It was just Chris and Keiko walking to the parking lot. Reo was going to Farid's for a sleepover.

"Let's go for pizza," Keiko said. "To celebrate."

"I'd love to, but I can't," said Chris. "I've got a big math test tomorrow. I should study."

"Come on, you deserve a break," said Keiko. "You played great. And we haven't talked in ages."

"I guess a quick slice wouldn't hurt," said Chris.

Chris was starving, and the pizza was delicious.

"Do you think you'll get invited to try out for the regional team?" asked Keiko.

"No, I don't have the skill," said Chris. "I'm a grinder. I make a lot of mistakes."

"But you've improved so much," said Keiko. "And you love playing."

"I do," said Chris. "More than I thought I would."

"I haven't seen you smile so much for months," she said.

"Yeah, I'm feeling pretty good," said Chris. "I hope it lasts."

The two talked and ate their pizza. When they were done, Keiko texted her dad to pick them up.

★ ★ ★

Holding Strong

When he got home, Chris spent only a short time studying. He figured he knew the math fairly well. But the test was much harder than he had expected. He failed it.

He sat staring at the big red *F* on his paper after his classmates and teacher had left the classroom. He was anxious. *Don't send me back into depression. Please, don't send me back. Please — Stop!* he told himself. *Stop! Next time, I'll use my last night before a test to study. And tomorrow, I'll talk to the teacher about writing a make-up test.* Chris grew calm and his anxiety faded.

After school, he met with Doctor Bhatt. He told her about the test and how he managed to calm himself. She replied that doing sports along with therapy would help him avoid relapses.

I've been playing soccer for six weeks, thought Chris. *And I think I'm handling things better.*

12 SCOUTED

"You guys have worked hard all season," said Coach Dave. "So whatever happens today, you can hold your heads high. Just play your best. That's all I can ask."

The team huddled and Luca led the cheer: "One! One! One for all! Move! Move! Move that ball! Challenge, Hotspurs!"

"Aren't you nervous about the scout?" Reo asked his teammates. "I am."

"No, not really," said Chris. "I've got no chance of making it, so why worry?"

"You've got that right," said Trent. "The guy would have to be as crazy as you to pick you."

Chris ignored Trent and took his place at centre field. The Hotspurs were playing the blue-shirted Fury. Chris had missed his team's game against the Fury early in the season. When he heard the score, he was thankful. The Hotspurs had lost five to nothing. *Maybe I can help us beat them this time*, he thought. *That's something to work towards.*

Scouted

The Hotspurs attacked. Noodin sent Luca a long pass. Luca crossed to Trent. Trent drilled a shot to the far corner. The Fury keeper dove and punched the ball out.

Trent ran down his own rebound. He turned and kicked.

The keeper was back up. He caught the shot.

Trent's on fire, Chris thought. *I'm sure he wants to make the regional team.*

Reo told Chris, "That keeper killed us last game. We had chances but he saved everything."

The Fury regrouped. They liked short passes, just like Coach Dave had taught the Hotspurs. Everyone moving, players shifting to open space. Teammates giving support. In no time the ball was in the Hotspurs end.

A Fury striker dribbled left, then right. To Chris it looked like he was dancing. Suddenly, the striker tapped the ball between Farid's legs and sped by. He was free. He dribbled in. The ball seemed to be attached to his feet.

Jake charged out of the net to make himself big to block the attack.

The striker saw him coming. Just in time he chipped the ball over Jake's head. The ball rose high, came down and rolled in.

Head down, Jake walked back to the net. He was mumbling to himself.

Chris hustled back. "Don't worry, bud. You had to risk it. He would have scored for sure."

"I know, but I almost had it," said Jake. "I hate to let one by. Even worse, I hate to let that keeper get the better of me."

Minutes later, Chris watched Luca run down the Fury midfielder. Luca challenged hard and stole the ball. Chris joined the attack. Luca passed to Chris. Chris sent the ball to Trent. Trent saw Reo charging the net and kicked the ball over. Reo leaped sideways, scissor kicking the ball while it was in the air. The keeper dove and blocked the shot with his elbow. Trent raced for the rebound, trying for an easy goal. A Fury defender beat him to it and booted the ball to safety.

"That keeper's killing us," moaned Reo. "Again."

The Fury broke out quick. The Hotspurs defenders were caught high. The Fury fullback sent the ball long. Their striker chased it down. He sped down the wing and picked the far corner.

Chris shook his head. It was frustrating to work so hard and then watch these guys pop one in.

The half ended with the Fury up by two.

Chris wiped the sweat from his head and arms. He took a long drink. He was hot and needed to hydrate.

"Man, that keeper's good," said Farid. "How are we going to beat him?"

"We need lots of shots," said Reo. "Have a go every chance we get."

"We can do this, boys," said Luca. "Leave everything on the field."

Chris was determined. *Time to focus on a goal*, he told himself. *And the goal is to win this game.* He ran hard to intercept a kickoff pass.

The Hotspurs worked the ball up the field.

Luca blasted a shot off the crossbar.

Reo aimed for the top corner. The keeper jumped and caught it.

The Fury keeper made save after save. The Hotspurs grew desperate.

Chris fought for the ball just outside the penalty area. A Fury defender bumped him hard. The referee gave the Hotspurs a direct kick. Farid took it quickly, curving the ball around the Fury's half-formed wall. Chris ran in and jumped high between three defenders. His head made contact and the ball zipped past the keeper, who was still moving the other way. Chris had narrowed the gap to one.

With five minutes left, the Hotspurs fought hard.

Luca stole balls. Trent blasted shots. Reo set up plays. Farid stopped attacks. But it wasn't enough. After Chris's goal, the Fury keeper saved every shot that came at him. The game ended and the Hotspurs' season was over.

"Awesome effort, guys!" said Coach Dave. "You tried your best. Every one of you. I couldn't be more proud. We just ran into one hot keeper."

The Comeback

"Yeah, we all know he'll be invited to the regional tryout," said Reo. He turned and saw Jake's sad face. "Along with Jake, of course."

"He got the best of me today," said Jake. "But I can't play in the Games anyway. We'll be on vacation."

Coach Dave pulled aside Chris, Reo, Farid, Trent and Luca. "Listen up, guys," he said. "The scout talked to me throughout the game. He was impressed with the five of you. He wants you to attend the Northern Central Regional Team tryout. I'll email you the details."

"I can't believe I've been invited," said Chris.

"I can't believe it either," said Trent.

"Now, now, Trent," said Coach Dave. "We Hotspurs support each other."

"Yeah, Chris, you deserve it," said Farid. "You played a solid game."

"He's played solid all season," said Reo.

"All I know is he makes a million mistakes," said Trent. "And has issues."

"The scout saw something in Chris," said Coach Dave. "Something I've seen all season. He's got character. He never gives up. He supports his teammates. He rallies the troops. Every team needs a guy like that."

Trent shrugged and looked away.

Chris felt proud. *I know I'm not the most skilled player,* he thought. *But I've got other things. The coach says I've got character.*

Scouted

Coach Dave walked with Chris back to the parking lot. "There's something you should know, Chris," he said. "The regional team coach is intense and competitive. He takes the game seriously and expects a lot. And he yells a lot. A lot more than me. Are you okay with that?"

"Yeah, that's all right."

"And everything's okay otherwise?" said Coach Dave. "You've been feeling good?"

"Yeah, I'm good. I love soccer," said Chris.

"That's great," said Coach Dave. "You know what sealed the deal for you? The scout told me."

"What?" said Chris.

"He told me it would have been so easy for you to give up. Down two to zero with an unbeatable keeper and only a few minutes left. But you didn't give up. You gave everything to try to come back."

"Everybody did," said Chris.

"Maybe so," said Coach Dave. "But you wanted it more. Everyone could see."

Everyone but Trent, thought Chris. He felt strong. He was too proud of his playing to let Trent bother him.

On the ride home, Chris told his dad about the game. Chris was so excited about how much fun he had playing that at first he forgot to mention that his team lost.

13 The TRYOUT

Chris wasn't nervous as he put on his cleats. *I've got nothing to lose*, he thought. *I didn't expect to be here. It's an honour that I was asked.*

He and Reo jogged onto the pitch and passed the ball. It was a sunny day, and there was a breeze.

"Wait till you see Coach Ron," said Reo. "He's one intense guy."

"Yeah, that's what Coach Dave told me," said Chris. "I like coaches that take the game seriously."

"Then he's the coach for you," said Reo. "I've had him for three years. Most of the time, he's great. But after one game, he got mad. He told us that we didn't pass. We didn't try. He held up the Most Valuable Player trophy that he was supposed to give someone and said, 'Not a single one of you deserves this.' Then he slammed the trophy into the garbage can."

"Wow," said Chris.

Reo went on. "My buddy turned to me and said, 'There goes your trophy, man. The team sucked, but you had a great game.' I'd been thinking I had a chance at getting the trophy. But no such luck."

"That's a bummer," said Chris.

Reo shook his head. "That's nothing," he said. "Two years ago we won bronze. We were the third-best team in Ontario. Not too shabby, eh? Everyone got a medal. After the game, Coach Ron held his medal high up in the air and said, 'Someday when you're old, you'll get this bronze hunk of metal out. And you'll remember what it's like to be a loser.'"

"Now that's way over the top," said Chris. "Why do you keep playing for him?"

"I love the Summer Games," said Reo. "And like I said, he's great most of the time. And he's getting better. Last year there weren't any incidents. I think he's calmed down."

"People can change," said Chris. "Maybe he has."

"I hope so," said Reo. "I like competitive coaches, too. But I'd rather not play for a wild man."

After warm-up, Coach Ron called everyone in. He was tall, tanned, bald and muscular.

Chris said hi to his former teammates Farid and Luca. He saw Trent but ignored him. *I know he deserves to be here*, Chris thought. *I just wish he was away and couldn't play, like Jake.* Chris saw Mini Messi in the crowd. The two exchanged smiles. He also saw Amare, the midfielder from the Titans. *All the best players in the league are here — and then some. I don't belong — Stop!*

Chris put that thought out of mind and vowed to do his best.

"First off, we're gonna work on dribbling," said Coach Ron. His voice was loud and gruff. "I've set up four runs of zigzagging pylons. Divide into four groups, one behind each run. I want you to dribble around each pylon in your run as fast as you can. When you hit each pylon, circle around it twice and continue on. The runs are close together — so keep your heads up. I don't want you bumping into players in the other runs."

Trent, Luca, Mini Messi and Amare were first in their lines. The whistle blew and they were off. Chris watched Luca take the lead on the way to the first pylon. He could dribble on the open field like no other. Mini Messi shot past him going around the second pylon. His foot control was superb. Trent wasn't far behind. He wasn't fast or showy, but he was always in control. Amare was smooth. He started slow but soon passed Trent. No one lost their ball or bumped into anyone.

Chris was next. The whistle blew and he raced off. His competitors were skilled. They passed him as they circled the first pylon and they kept ahead. Chris picked up his speed to try to catch up. He lost control of the ball and crossed into another run to get it. His head was down and he ran hard into a dribbler.

"Heyyyy!" roared Coach Ron. "What in the world are you doing? If you lose control and race blindly into another run, someone's gonna get hurt. Keep your head up! Keep control!"

Chris was startled. He jumped back. He'd never been scolded so harshly for one mistake. *Wait*, he told himself. *A little yelling on the field never hurt anyone.* He slowed down to keep the ball at his feet. As he dribbled back, he realized, *It's a safety issue. I've got to do better.*

The one-on-one drill was next. A line of attackers and a line of defenders. One attacker would try to score in one of three nets of pylons set up in a square. Chris had to go against Farid. *How am I going to break through his wall?* wondered Chris.

Chris came at Farid. He moved left and suddenly shifted right. Farid wasn't fooled. The defender challenged hard and kicked the ball out of bounds.

A few turns later, Chris had to defend against Mini Messi. Mini Messi came at him quick. His foot circled the ball so many times, Chris's head was spinning. Mini Messi danced away and tapped the ball between a two-pylon net.

Coach Ron kept the boys moving all afternoon. Four drills later, Chris was exhausted. *But I feel good*, thought Chris. *It's not like the weariness of depression. It's a good kind of exhausted from effort.* In one drill, Chris had headed the ball well. In another, he'd sent Luca a couple of nice passes. Now it was time for the eight-on-eight half-field scrimmages.

Chris was on a squad with Farid and six guys he

didn't know. Trent was teamed up with Luca, Reo, Mini Messi, Amare and three talented kids. *The soccer gods aren't on my side today*, thought Chris. *That other squad is stacked.*

Trent's squad came on strong. They were a skilled machine and controlled the ball for long periods. Farid and Chris defended hard. Challenge after challenge. Tackle after tackle. It wasn't pretty, but Chris and Farid shut down the stars.

With seconds left, Chris challenged Trent hard and stole the ball. Trent looked to Coach Ron for the yellow card — it didn't come. Chris dribbled in and Farid joined the rush. Chris crossed the ball and Farid kicked it in.

"Awesome job, guys," hollered Coach Ron. "You found a way."

After the other two squads scrimmaged, everyone gathered on the sidelines and waited for Coach Ron to make his decisions.

Chris was too hot and tired to be nervous. *I've got nothing to lose*, he repeated to himself. He noticed Reo pacing back and forth. Luca looked confident. *Why not?* thought Chris. *He's a great player.*

Trent sneered at Chris. "You're lucky there wasn't a ref," he told Chris. "He would've given you six yellow cards."

"You've always got an excuse, don't you, Trent?" said Chris.

The Tryout

"Coach Ron was watching the scrimmage," said Farid. "He didn't say anything."

"That guy lets everything go," said Trent.

Finally, Coach Ron was ready. He read the list of the players he'd chosen for the Northern Central Regional Team. It included Mini Messi, Luca, Trent, Reo, Farid, the keeper from the Fury, Amare, seven guys Chris didn't know — and Chris.

Chris couldn't believe it. He was going to the Summer Games!

As Chris was getting ready to leave, Coach Ron took him aside. "You're one determined kid," he said. "I wasn't sure if I should pick you. So I stacked the squad against you and your friend in the scrimmage to see what you can do. I don't know how, but you beat my best players. It's great to have you."

"Thanks, Coach," said Chris. "I'm looking forward to playing." He realized that he really was.

"I'm glad you made it, Chris," said Reo as they left the field. "You really came through in that scrimmage."

"Farid did most of the work," said Chris.

"Enough with the modesty!" said Reo. "You need to strut your stuff."

Chris smiled. "That's not my style."

"We'll have a great time anyway," said Reo. "Are you gonna tell the team about your . . . situation?"

"About my depression?"

"Yeah, sorry to ask. I'm just wondering."

"Nah, I don't think so," said Chris after thinking for a second. "I've been feeling good. No recent relapses. Why, do you think I should?"

"No, not really," said Reo. He checked his pockets and soccer bag. "I think I forgot my sunglasses. I better head back. They're expensive."

Chris headed to the lot for his ride. He tried walking a little taller — strutting his stuff. *This is silly*, he thought. *The only place to show your stuff is on the pitch*.

14 SPURNED

Chris stood with Reo and Farid on the field beside the track at Varsity Stadium in downtown Toronto. He couldn't believe how many athletes were taking part. He figured there were at least two thousand, and one or two thousand spectators. The young competitors were wearing their team uniforms or sports clothes. Chris felt the energy in the air.

Chris saw Ben, his new team's keeper, behind him. It was the goalie who had stood on his head to win the league semi-final match. "Isn't this awesome?" said Chris.

Ben said nothing and turned away quickly.

I guess he didn't hear me, thought Chris.

Music began to play and the athletes started their march. Sport by sport, they were to walk around the track. First up in alphabetical order were the archers, walking behind a girl holding an archery sign. Then came three huge groups — athletics, baseball and basketball. More than a dozen sports followed.

Soccer was way down the alphabet, so it was fifteen

minutes before Chris and his teammates stepped onto the track. Soon they were passing by the spectators — family members, friends and fans. As the athletes passed, the audience cheered, whistled and waved. Chris and his teammates waved back. Chris looked up at the adoring crowd. *This must be like how it feels to be a celebrity*, he thought.

As the athletes finished their walk, they veered onto the grass in front of the stage on the other side of the stadium. Dusk was coming and Chris took in the Toronto skyline. So different from Parry Sound. But so beautiful.

Everyone socialized as they waited for the opening ceremony. Players from different soccer teams chatted. Kids from different sports mingled. It was a noisy, diverse, vibrant scene.

Chris tapped Mini Messi on the shoulder. "Hey, man, can you believe this crowd?"

Mini Messi half-smiled and moved away.

Chris turned to Reo. "Do I have B.O. or something?"

"No, why?" asked Reo.

"Nobody seems to want to talk to me," said Chris.

Reo looked like he was about to speak. But then he stopped.

Farid jumped in. "Don't worry, bro! I'll talk to you whether you stink or not."

The opening ceremony began with a rousing "O Canada" by a singer Chris knew from the internet. Then there were speeches by an Ontario government minister and an elite Canadian sprinter. Another athlete lit a torch and ran with it along the track. He passed it to another athlete who ran a little ways and passed it to a third. The three runners represented Opportunity, Inspiration and Community. The third athlete took the torch to a tall Summer Games cauldron and lit a roaring flame.

When the government minister announced that the Ontario Summer Games were open, everyone in the stadium cheered. *All right*, thought Chris. *Now it's time to play.*

★ ★ ★

The Northern Central Regional Team's first game was against Oakville. Chris and his teammates had been together only two weeks and had practised just four times. The Oakville players looked like a team that had played together all season.

Coach Ron announced the starting lineup. It included Chris and the four other Hotspurs players, plus Ben the keeper, Amare and Mini Messi, and Santos, Cruz and Tim. Four teammates filled out the roster on the sideline: Bailey, Alan, Jacob and Max.

Five minutes in, Chris passed to the open space where he thought Amare, playing midfield, would run. Amare ran the other way. These guys ran different patterns than Chris was used to. He approached Amare to discuss the play. Amare smiled but didn't reply.

Midway through the first half, Oakville kept control. With sharp passing, they moved the ball deep into Northern Central's end. Farid angled his opponent into the corner and knocked the ball out of bounds. It was a corner kick for Oakville.

An Oakville midfielder took the kick. He ran at the ball. Instead of kicking towards the net, he passed the ball back to a nearby forward. A short corner to give the forward a better angle from which to direct his kick. He kicked hard towards the net. An Oakville striker jumped high and headed the ball into the net.

At halftime, Chris sought out Mini Messi. "Hey, you want to gather a few of the new guys? We need to talk about our plays. We aren't used to each other."

"Don't you worry, Chris," said Mini Messi. "It will all work out." And he was gone.

I don't understand, thought Chris. *Mini Messi and the new guys were all friendly during the tryout. Now none of them are talking to me. It doesn't make sense. They seem scared.*

In the second half, Chris lost confidence. Passes went wild. His challenges were weak. He got beaten to loose balls. *I just don't know how to read these new guys*, he thought. *And none of them will talk to me to make things right.*

With ten minutes left, Luca set up Chris in scoring position. *At least we Hotspurs still know what one another is doing*, thought Chris. It was the perfect time to bend the ball. Then Chris remembered that he had meant to ask Farid for tips on how to do it. But he had never got around to it. Chris tried anyway. He drove the top of his foot through the lower half of the ball. The ball spun wildly and rose and rose. Again, Chris had struck from too far under. The ball flew high over the crossbar.

"Another field goal?" sneered Trent. "If you can't bend the ball, why do you keep trying?"

Chris shrugged and followed Trent to the touchline.

"Coach, you've gotta sub Chris," said Trent. "He's going to cost us the game."

"You can take me out if you want, Coach," said Chris. "Nothing's working today."

"Or any other day," said Trent.

"I'll have none of that, young man," snapped Coach Ron. "Or you'll be the one sitting. It's just Summer Games nerves. All of you are caught up with the pomp and big crowds. Once you settle down and get used to each other, you'll be fine."

I'm not so sure we'll be fine, thought Chris. *For some reason, no one's talking to me.*

Things didn't get better. Northern Central's passes kept going wild. The team's forwards raced around the field blindly. No one talked to each other. No one knew where their teammates were. The last ten minutes passed without one good chance, and Oakville won.

Chris left the field confused. *I'll have to have a chat with Reo*, he told himself. *Maybe he can explain what's going on. We can't afford to lose any more games.*

15 FEAR

Back at the hotel, Chris sat watching sports highlights with Reo and Farid in Farid's room. Chris figured it was now or never.

"Guys, did you notice anything weird last game?" he asked.

"Like what?" said Reo.

"The new guys weren't passing to me," said Chris. "They weren't even talking to me."

"Yeah, I noticed," said Farid. "Maybe it's because they aren't used to playing with you."

"I think it's more than that," said Chris. "I don't know what. Can you think of anything?"

Chris looked to his friends. *Reo knows something*, he thought. *Last game, he started to say something and stopped.* "Reo, what's up, bro? You know everything around here."

Chris watched as Reo's face lit up as a thought came to him.

"Yeah, I think I know what's up," said Reo.

"What?" asked Chris.

"Remember after the tryout — when I forgot my sunglasses and went back for them?"

Chris nodded.

"When I got to the field, Trent was talking to the new guys," said Reo. "I looked for my sunglasses and listened in. He was telling them how depressed you are and how it affects your mood and play."

"But that's not true," said Chris. "I've been feeling okay for weeks. And I've been playing all right."

"You've been playing better than all right," offered Farid.

"Did he say anything else?" Chris asked Reo.

"Oh, he went on about how you cost the Hotspurs the league semi-final," said Reo.

"That's not true, either," said Chris.

"Not at all," said Reo.

"We wouldn't have made it there without you," said Farid.

"Yeah," Reo agreed. "Trent even told the new guys that he's worried about what you might do if we don't win the gold medal."

"Like what?" said Chris.

"You don't want to know," said Reo. "It's that stupid."

"Come on, Reo," said Chris. "I need to know."

"He said he's worried you might try to commit suicide if we don't win gold," said Reo. "He told them to be careful around you. And to watch what they say.

He said anything might set you off."

"Unbelievable," said Chris. "All lies. How's a team supposed to learn to play together when half the players are scared to talk to a teammate? And won't pass to him?"

"I don't think Trent thinks he's lying," said Reo. "I think he believes that nonsense. He still doesn't understand depression."

"Maybe I should set everyone straight," said Chris. "The last time I came clean, it worked out well — on everyone but Trent."

"I think that's a good idea," said Reo.

"Me, too," said Farid. "When people have the facts, they usually do the right thing. And some guys need to hear things a couple of times before it sinks in. Guys like Trent."

"I'm sorry I didn't tell you before, Chris," said Reo. "I was hoping no one would listen to Trent."

"That's okay," said Chris. "I should have told them from the beginning."

"I wouldn't say that," said Farid. "It wasn't an issue till Trent made it one. You couldn't have known he'd do that."

"I guess you're right," said Chris. "I just hope there's time to get this team working together."

★ ★ ★

That evening, Chris told Coach Ron about his

depression. And about how the teammates who didn't know him were scared to talk to him or pass to him. It wasn't easy. Chris knew the coach could be gruff.

When Chris was done, Coach Ron cleared his throat.

Chris didn't know what to expect. For all he knew, Coach was going to cut him from the team.

"I'm gonna tell you something, Chris," said the coach. "Something that I've never told any of my players. I used to have a problem controlling my anger. I'd get so mad when the boys played badly that I'd yell my head off and say stupid things. I didn't do it often, but it was often enough. And it wasn't the way I wanted to be. So I spoke with an anger management counsellor. He taught me to think before I speak. To wait until I was calm and then express my anger and look for solutions. And he showed me a few relaxation techniques. I found that talking to him, and to my life partner, and even other coaches, helped a lot. I got the things that were bothering me off my chest and learned coping strategies. I think you letting the boys know about your illness is a great idea. How did they find out, anyway? I hadn't noticed anything."

"Oh, they must have heard it through the grapevine," said Chris. Chris wanted to set the record straight, but he didn't want to get Trent in trouble. *I just want the guy to understand*, he thought. *This is his last chance.*

"Well, son, I admire your honesty," said Coach Ron. "I'll call a meeting for tomorrow morning and let everyone know. And if anyone gives you a hard time, you let me know. I won't put up with that kind of thing."

That was easier than I expected, thought Chris.

The next morning after breakfast, everyone gathered in Coach Ron's hotel room. "It's come to my attention," said the coach, "that many of you have heard Chris has depression. And that you're scared to pass to him and talk to him. Well, Chris has something to say. Please listen up. This is important."

Chris stood at the back of the room by the window. Tim, Cruz and Santos were perched on the bed. The others were spread around the room. Coach Ron was sitting in the armchair like a king on his throne.

"Several months ago, I got depressed," said Chris. "It came out of nowhere, and it got worse when I got injured. Since then, I've been seeing a psychologist and getting therapy. Part of that has been learning not to blame myself for everything. Part has been playing soccer. It's going well. I love soccer. I'm feeling better. I've never tried to hurt myself and I'm sure I never will. Depression is a disease. It isn't as simple as just being sad. It affects everything I do. Sometimes I feel like every part of my body is sad and I'm carrying a heavy weight." Chris went on, "But most people who have it aren't violent. They don't need to be feared. With proper care, they go to school, work and play sports like everyone else. So you've got nothing to worry about — except playing together and trying to play our best."

Fear

Coach Ron stood up. "Thanks for that, Chris. You've got guts," he said. "Those are the facts, everyone. Chris isn't going to kill himself if you say something wrong or look at him the wrong way. Or if we don't win gold. It doesn't work like that. He's taken the steps to get his disease under control. And from what I can see, he's a vital part of this team. So let's turn this around, guys. There's still time. I need you talking out there and passing. I need you supporting each other. Can you do that?"

The team roared in approval.

"Good, let's do it then," said Coach Ron. "Today we play Burlington. Let's show them what we're made of."

Chris watched the coach tap Trent's shoulder as Trent went by. "You didn't have anything to do with spreading all that fear, did you, son?"

Trent shrugged. "This is a regional team. It's supposed to be the best players giving their best. Chris may not hurt himself or anyone, but can he really give his best?"

"I think he can," said Coach Ron. "Just give him a chance. Can you do that?"

"I'll try, Coach," said Trent. "Even though I'm not sure it'll work."

Well, at least the guy's gonna try, thought Chris.

Mini Messi stopped Chris on his way out. "Great speech. I didn't know any of that. Sorry for listening to the rumours. I should have known better."

"No problem, man," said Chris. "We're back on track."

16 Bad CALLS

Chris, Farid and Reo arrived early for the second game. Ben, the keeper, had just finished stretching.

"Hey, Farid, can you give me some tips on bending the ball?" asked Chris. "I've been meaning to ask you and keep forgetting. And then embarrassing myself on the field."

"Of course, my friend," said Farid. "I'm the master."

"Yeah, master of the swollen heads," kidded Reo.

"You may be right," said Farid. "But I'll straighten out Chris. Or should I say, I'll unstraighten him."

The boys lined up by the penalty spot and Ben took the net.

"Have a try," said Farid. "Let me see how you do it."

Chris lined up at a ninety-degree angle. He took three steps and kicked hard. The ball hardly spun and didn't curve. It flew high over the net, as usual. Ben didn't even move. He could tell the shot was going high the whole time.

"I see a few things," said Farid. "I like to approach the ball at a forty-five-degree angle. You're hitting the

94

ball too low. Yes, you want to hit low to raise the ball. But you don't want to get right under like a chip shot."

Chris tried another shot. He approached at forty-five degrees and kicked the ball a little higher. The ball didn't curve much, but it was on net. Ben had to move quickly to make the save.

"Much better," said Farid.

"That had some pepper!" shouted Ben.

"You're getting there," said Reo.

"Two more things," added Farid. "You're not getting your body over the ball. You're leaning back. When you lean back, you lose power and the ball goes high. You're also not getting spin. You have to swing your leg around as you kick. Try another."

Chris did everything Farid said. There was so much to remember, he didn't hit the ball as hard as usual. Chris watched as it shot towards the net and spun slowly left. Ben had lots of time to make the save — but the ball had curved.

"Nice one, Chris!" hollered Ben.

"Awesome," said Reo.

"Good curve," praised Farid. "You're coming along. Now you have to hit the ball with more power. The harder you hit, the more spin you'll get."

"Yeah, have you ever seen videos of Beckham's free kicks?" asked Reo. "The ball seems to bend faster as it gets closer to the net."

"He's incredible," said Farid.

"And you're not too bad a teacher," said Reo.

"Thanks!" said Farid. "While I'm at it, what would *you* like to learn?"

The boys laughed and took turns practising. With each kick, Chris got a little better. The ball wasn't bending as much as he'd like, but it was bending. And it was on net. A little more work and he might just get it right.

★ ★ ★

Burlington came on strong in the first half. They had lots of chances. Ben had to stand on his head to keep the game scoreless. Just like he'd done to beat the Hotspurs in the league semi-final.

The Burlington forwards were aggressive. The midfielders were playing high. Even the defenders were joining the attack. One ran in and received a cross pass. Chris ran with him. At the last second, he launched a slide tackle and knocked the ball to safety. The ref blew the whistle and gave Burlington a penalty kick.

"But I got the ball," said Chris.

"And his ankle," said the ref.

"No, I didn't," said Chris.

The ref ignored him. The Burlington fullback took the penalty kick. He drilled the ball low into the left corner of the net.

"I can't believe it," said Chris. "That was a bad call."

Bad Calls

"Zip it," said Trent. "The last thing we need is a yellow card."

Chris felt himself get angry. *What a horrible call*, he thought. *I got all ball.* He took a deep breath. *I've got to keep my cool*, he told himself. *We're down a goal in a must-win game.*

Chris worked to win a loose ball in the attacking zone. He was with Mini Messi with only one defender back. Chris watched as Mini Messi started his run. Chris timed his pass perfectly as Mini Messi raced past the defender and into the ball.

The whistle blew again. Offside.

"That wasn't offside," said Chris.

The ref ignored him. It was Burlington's ball.

"Incredible," jeered Chris. He was about to stomp the grass with his cleats. He stopped himself.

The ref glared at Chris.

"Keep your feelings to yourself, Chris," said Trent. "You're gonna cost us the game."

Chris knew Trent was right. But this ref wasn't making it easy. Chris looked to Coach Ron on the sideline. The coach had his hands in the air but was keeping calm.

During halftime, Chris wiped the sweat from his face and poured water over his head. Anything to cool down the heat — and the frustration. He ate a few pieces of orange and promised himself that he'd remain calm. *If Coach Ron can do it, so can I*, thought Chris.

"That ref's cheap," said Reo. "He's gonna give them the game."

"I know," said Chris. "But we've got to play through it."

Early in the second half, Luca ran towards a loose ball. A Burlington defender wanted it, too. Neither gave any ground. The two players crashed into each other, and the smaller Burlington player tumbled down.

The whistle blew and out came a yellow card. The ref cautioned Luca.

"What the heck?" said Trent. He approached the ref. "They ran into each other! Are you out —"

Chris pulled Trent back. He was surprised that Trent was losing his cool. But the call was ridiculous. Both players were responsible. The only reason the Burlington kid fell was that he was smaller.

Chris patted Trent's shoulder. "Don't worry, man. We can do this." Chris felt his own frustration fade as he worked to calm his teammate.

A few minutes later, Chris sent Luca a pass in the penalty area. Luca stretched out his leg to kick the ball, but he missed. The fullback who came to defend tripped over Luca's outstretched leg. The whistle blew. The ref waved a red card. Luca — the cleanest player Chris knew — was thrown out of the game. Northern Central would have to play the rest of the game a man down.

Chris began to lose hope. *We can't win playing a*

man short, he thought. He wanted to challenge the ref, but held back. *I've got to fight this feeling of already being defeated,* he told himself. *This isn't my fault. It isn't the team's fault. It's a bad referee. Everyone's down and I've got to do something. I've got to rally the team.*

"Look, boys," Chris said. "Don't worry about the ref. We're only down a goal and we've got time. We can do this — for Luca."

"You bet we can," roared Farid.

"I'm with you," said Mini Messi.

"Chris is right," said Trent. "Let's do it for Luca."

"For Luca!" Northern Central cheered.

Minutes later, Chris intercepted a pass. He sent the ball wide to Mini Messi. Mini Messi had three men on him. Somehow the gifted striker danced by all three and dribbled in on goal. The keeper came out to cut down the angle. Mini Messi had one move left. He feinted left and pushed the ball right. The keeper was beat and Mini Messi booted the ball into the open net.

The game was tied.

Burlington came back strong and blasted a shot just wide. Ben placed the ball for the goal kick and hoofed it two thirds down the field to Trent. Trent passed to Chris. Chris dropped it back to Reo. Reo gave it to Farid. And Farid drove a long, curving bullet into the top corner. Northern Central had won!

"I guess those practice shots paid off," said Farid.

"For you — not for me," joked Chris.

The Comeback

"You'll get your chance one day," said Reo.

"Yeah, in the senior recreation league," said Chris.

As Chris left the field, Trent nodded his way. "Thanks for calming me down out there. I almost lost my head."

"No worries," Chris said with surprise. "It happens to the best of them." *I don't believe it*, he thought. *Maybe I'm getting through to Trent.*

17 The COMEBACK KID

Ottawa South United was a skilled team. Northern Central had to beat them to advance to the semi-final. So far Chris's team had won one and lost one. They couldn't afford to lose or tie their last round–robin match.

Chris was pumped. It felt good to have rallied the team to beat Burlington. *And we did it playing a man short*, thought Chris. *Best of all, I proved to Trent that I can control my emotions. I even helped Trent control his.*

For ten minutes, Northern Central hardly touched the ball. Ottawa South played a possession game — they kept control, making lots of passes. Chris and his teammates were constantly chasing the ball. As soon as they got close, their opponents would pass the ball away. *We've got to play smarter*, thought Chris. *But how?*

Ottawa South worked their way down the field.

Chris covered his man. It felt like all he could do was watch as Ottawa South worked the ball. *These guys are good at everything*, he thought. *Smooth first touches. Perfect traps. Moves when they need them.*

The Comeback

The ball was deep in the corner in Northern Central's end. Reo challenged the striker. The striker made a short pass. Farid challenged the new attacker. The attacker made a pass. Cruz challenged the guy who received the pass. The guy chipped a pass outside the box. The Ottawa South centre volleyed the ball with his foot. He turned around quickly and walloped the ball out of the air with his same foot. Ben didn't have a chance as the ball ripped into the corner.

"I've never seen anyone do that before," said Reo.

"I'm not even sure I know what he did," said Farid.

"Yeah, we'll have to study that one in slo-mo," said Luca.

"If only we could," said Chris. "I'd love to see it again."

As the half wound down, Chris and his teammates grew tired from chasing their opponents. With one minute left, Ottawa South's centre midfielder took advantage of it. He trapped a pass out of mid-air with his foot and went for a run. His first touch set the ball beyond his defender. He ran past the defender and dribbled on. He pushed the ball right, racing by Farid. He beat the last defender and shot hard, catching the keeper going the other way.

Ottawa South was up two to nothing at halftime.

Chris sat with his teammates drinking water and eating oranges.

"How can we score if we can't get the ball?" said Farid.

"It's so frustrating," said Reo. "I feel like I'm one

of the spectators."

Coach Ron called the team over. "These guys control the ball well," he said. "And they're highly skilled. We need to mark our men better, close down the passing lanes and have one man attack the ball aggressively. But only one man — the rest of you have got to shut down the passing lanes. The pressure will force the attacker to pass before he's ready. With their men covered and the passing lanes closed, we should win some balls."

Chris wanted gold. *That's why we're here*, he thought. *But for us to win, I've got to make something happen.* When his man got the ball, he challenged fiercely. He forced a wild pass and Farid ran to the ball. Farid passed to Jacob, who launched it to Chris. Chris found himself clear in scoring range. *Bend-it-like-Beckham time*, he thought. He took a shot. It curved nicely.

The keeper shuffled right to make the save.

Chris shook his head in frustration. He saw Trent approaching and waited for the jibe.

"Getting there," said Trent. "Keep them coming."

Trent encouraging me? thought Chris. He was speechless.

Slowly, Northern Central gained control more often. Luca attacked hard and forced turnovers. Mini Messi used his speed to intercept hurried passes.

Chris saw that Amare was joining the rush and was often open. Chris dribbled in from the side and passed it across. Amare one-timed the ball into the net.

"Nice pass," said Amare.

"Nice finish," said Chris.

At centre field, Luca intercepted a pass. He kicked the ball to Chris and ran. Chris led Luca with a pass. Luca ran into the ball and dribbled in. Chris could see the centre's fire. He wasn't as fancy as Ottawa South's centre. But when he bore ahead full speed with the ball, he was hard to stop. Stretching his long legs and racing ahead, Luca found an opening to shoot. He drilled the ball low into the right corner.

The game was tied with four minutes left.

Ottawa South came on strong. They had the skill to play at a new level. Ben caught balls, punched balls and dove madly to make save after save. He kept Northern Central in the game.

With one minute left, Chris and Trent rushed down the right side. Trent passed to Chris. Chris passed it back.

Chris could see that the keeper was way out of his net. "Shoot! Shoot!" he yelled.

Trent looked up to aim and rifled a long, hard volley. The ball soared over everyone's heads. The keeper raced back. The ball came down out of his reach and dropped into the net.

There was no time for celebration. There was work to do. They had to keep their lead.

Right after kickoff, Luca stole a loose ball. He

passed it back to Reo. To kill time, Reo passed it back to Farid. Farid dribbled to the side and the whistle blew.

Northern Central was off to the semi-finals.

Everyone rushed in to hug Trent.

Trent smiled and cheered. When the crowd broke up, he told everyone, "Chris did all the work. He got us back into it."

"Just like he rallied us last game," said Farid.

"It's becoming a habit," said Reo. "Maybe we should call you the Comeback Kid."

Chris shook his head. He'd been called worse things in his life. Only a few months ago, he was hiding in washrooms and couldn't get out of bed. Now he was off to the semis in the Ontario Summer Games.

18 HEATWAVE

Reo wiped the sweat from his forehead. "Man, we're playing the semi on the hottest day of the summer."

"Well, it is the Ontario *Summer* Games," said Chris.

"You guys think this is hot?" said Farid. "Back in Syria we used to play in the scorching heat. I could fry eggs on the cement in the parking lot."

"What about falafel?" asked Reo.

Farid laughed. "Maybe," he said. "You know I wouldn't want to skip my falafel."

Coach Ron gathered his team. "You've come a long way in a short time, boys. Remember to talk out there. Support your teammates. And whatever you do, make sure you stay hydrated. It's a hot one."

"Coach, I'm not feeling too good," said Ben, holding his head.

Everyone turned to the keeper. He sat down on the grass.

Coach Ron hurried to his side. "What's wrong, Ben?"

"I'm feeling dizzy, tired. And like I might throw up," said the keeper. "I had a good sleep. I don't know what's wrong."

"Sounds like a mild case of heat exhaustion," said the coach. "You need to sit in the shade for a while and drink lots of water. Do you have a hat?"

"Yeah," moaned Ben. "But I have to play. I can't let the team down."

"Soak your hat in water, Ben. Then put it on to cool yourself off," said Coach Ron. "You won't be letting the team down. Amare, you play goal too, right?"

"Yeah, I love to play goal," said Amare. "But I'm nowhere near as good as Ben."

"Well, do your best," said the coach. "As soon as Ben's feeling better, we'll put him back in."

Coach Ron asked a dad who was a nurse to tend to Ben. Chris watched as the dad walked the keeper to a shady spot. He felt his forehead and gave him an ice pack. Chris was glad the keeper was in good hands. *But can we beat Richmond Hill without him?* he thought. *Ben can steal games.*

Richmond Hill started with the ball. Chris noticed that their style was different from Ottawa South's. Ottawa South had made lots of short passes and controlled the ball. Richmond Hill was more aggressive. The team made long passes to breaking strikers.

The Comeback

One Richmond Hill attacker trapped a long pass. The ball fell to his feet and he took off down the side. Reo tried but couldn't catch him. Bailey, on right fullback, joined the chase. The attacker turned and shifted abruptly right. He headed for the net, leaving Bailey behind. Farid came out to meet him. The attacker pushed the ball to Farid's right. He sped past Farid to the rolling ball. He turned and kicked for the corner.

Amare dove and got a piece of the ball. The rebound bounced out to the Richmond Hill centre. He blasted the ball past the fallen keeper for the first goal of the game.

Farid consoled Amare. "Don't worry, bud. That one's not your fault. I should have had that guy."

"No, no, Farid," said Reo. "It's not your fault either. I should have had him."

"Well, someone should have had him," said Trent. "He just ran through you all."

Luca glared at Trent. "I didn't see you stopping him," he said.

"Come on, guys," said Chris. "It's no one's fault. We just have to back each other up."

Richmond Hill didn't let up. *It's like Amare is in a mad shooting gallery*, thought Chris. The keeper punched a corner kick heading for the top corner out to safety. He charged an attacking striker who rushed in on a breakaway. The two collided and Farid cleared the loose ball. And before the half ended, Amare dove to save a sure goal.

Sweating buckets, the boys hurried off the field for water and oranges.

"Man, you're keeping us in this game," Chris told Amare.

"I just wish I could get back that one they got," said the keeper. "It's killing me."

"Don't sweat it," said Luca. "You're playing well."

"It's hard not to sweat it on a day like this," joked Reo.

Chris knew that Amare was playing well. But a shot had to go in soon. Richmond Hill was getting too many chances. Not only did the team need Ben in goal, they also needed Amare in the midfield.

Near the end of halftime, Chris watched as Coach Ron approached the nurse looking after Ben. They chatted for a minute. Coach Ron motioned for Ben to get up. The keeper took off his hat and started walking towards the team with the coach.

"I've got great news, guys," said Coach Ron. "Ben has been cleared to play."

"All right!" Chris said pumping his fist. His teammates cheered, too.

The coach smiled and said, "Amare, thanks for keeping us in this one. You did us proud. Remember boys, tag your men close. And look for that long pass. These guys won't know what to do if their forwards are covered. And if we're lucky, we'll steal some of those long balls."

Northern Central started the second half slowly and built momentum. Luca dribbled in for a look and a try. The keeper caught the ball and hoofed it down the field.

Amare intercepted a long pass and fed the ball to Trent. Trent crossed to Chris, who was in scoring range. Chris hit the ball low — but not too low — and followed through, just like Farid had taught him. The ball whizzed in and curved right! It bounced off the post.

Chris shook his head in disbelief.

"Sooooo close, Chris," said Reo. "You're getting the hang of it."

"Yeah, I might put one in sometime in the 2030s," said Chris.

"Or the decade after that," said Trent.

Is he joking? Chris wondered. *With Trent, you just never know. Either way, I can't lose hope. My teammates haven't. They're challenging. They're taking risks.*

With six minutes left, Luca dribbled up the field. Chris could again see the fire in his eyes. The tall centre charged down the wing. He cut inside with speed and raced to the net.

The fullback challenged hard. Luca turned, using his long legs to keep the ball out of the defender's reach. When Luca saw Reo charging in, he passed the ball over. With deadly accuracy, Reo shot into the top corner.

The game was tied.

After the kickoff, Chris raced in to steal the ball. Instead of passing to Trent or Reo, he dished it to Amare. *He's going to want to make up for the goal he let in,* thought Chris. *What better motivation could there be?*

Chris ran ahead of Amare and took the return pass. He dribbled deep into Richmond Hill's end and waited. *Amare's going to be joining the rush,* he thought. *Here he comes.* Chris lifted a cross pass high into the box.

Amare came running at full speed. He made a higher jump than anyone Chris had ever seen. Amare's head rose above those of the tall defenders. His forehead made contact with the ball and sent it zipping into the net.

"I never would have dreamed those short legs could jump so high, Amare," said Reo. "And I should know — I've got short legs, too."

With two minutes left, Richmond Hill turned up the pressure. Farid knocked the ball out of bounds, which gave their opponents a corner kick. The whole Richmond Hill team, including the keeper, lined up in and around the goal area. They had to score, and score now.

The stocky fullback kicked the ball high towards the net. It was a beauty, but Ben caught it. He hoofed the ball way down the field to Chris. Chris dribbled in and timed a perfect pass to Trent. Trent ran past the last defender to the ball.

Trent had a breakaway on an open net.

He dribbled towards the goal.

Chris joined Trent on the rush and ran interference. He waited for Trent to shoot the ball into the net.

But Trent didn't shoot. A few yards from the net, he passed to Chris and motioned for him to shoot it in.

Chris was shocked. What did Trent want him to do? The Richmond Hill defender was rushing in, so at the last moment Chris came to his senses. He kicked the ball into the empty net.

"You deserved one, Chris," said Trent. He came to thump Chris on the back. "You came to play."

"Thanks, man," said Chris. "You really scared me there. I didn't know what you were doing."

Seconds later the whistle blew. Chris and Trent were swarmed by their teammates.

Northern Central was off to the final.

19 The FINAL

"These North Mississauga guys look good," said Farid. "I just saw one put a warm-up shot into the top corner from the centre line."

"The guy with the shiny green cleats that glow in the dark?" asked Ben.

"Yeah, that's him," said Farid.

"North Mississauga's good, all right," said Reo. "They've won gold here the past two years."

"Don't worry, boys," said Chris. "We're good, too."

During warm-up drills, Chris looked to the stands. They were packed. His parents were there, and so were Keiko and Coach Dave. Even Doctor Bhatt had come out. They were all sitting together. Chris waved and they waved back.

It was a beautiful day — nowhere near as hot as the day of the semi. *I can't believe I'm here*, thought Chris. *It's everything I've worked towards.*

North Mississauga started on attack.

The Comeback

Chris waited for the first touch of the ball. He was nervous. More nervous than usual. *That's expected*, he thought. *This is the gold medal game. But I'm not anxious or panicked.*

North Mississauga worked the ball into Northern Central's end. Their passes were precise. With only one or two touches, the ball was placed under control and moved on.

A North Mississauga striker came at Chris.

Chris positioned himself well.

With the outside of his left foot, the striker tapped the ball outside to his left. He used his left foot again to pull the ball back and tapped it with his heel in the opposite direction. Then, with his right foot, he pulled the ball in the opposite direction. He finished by tapping the ball forward with his left foot.

Chris stood with his jaw hanging open as the striker raced past him.

"I don't believe it," said Reo. "The Rivaldo! I've never seen anyone do it so well at our level."

The striker dribbled in and passed the ball. North Mississauga passed five more times before the centre blasted a kick. Ben raced across the goal line to catch the ball in his stomach.

North Mississauga continued to pound the net with shots. As usual, Ben made save after save. Then, with one minute left in the half, the ball came to the guy with the shiny green cleats. He was in the box with his back to the goal. He jumped and, with a bicycle kick, shot the ball backwards over his head. The ball went into the net before the player came crashing down.

Chris shook his head in frustration.

At halftime, Coach Ron gathered his team. "These guys are good," he said. "Very good. But we can beat them. What we have to do is take away their time and space. Tag your men well. Challenge hard. And don't give an inch. All the moves in the world won't do you any good if you don't have any space to make them in."

Slowly, Northern Central's good defence wore North Mississauga down. The attackers were still doing the fancy footwork, but they had nowhere to go. They were making pass after pass, but never got a clear shot. All their skill was on display, but they couldn't finish. When they did get a shot, Ben would make the save.

At the midpoint of the second half, Luca stole the ball off shiny green cleats. The guy looked exhausted from dancing across the field. For the third time in the Games, Chris saw the fire in Luca's eyes. The tall centre took off down the field, daring anyone to get in his way.

Two defenders came at him. Luca pushed the ball between them and raced right through. The goalie charged out. Luca waited for him to dive for the ball and then pushed it away with his long leg. Luca dribbled two steps and smashed the ball into the net.

The Comeback

Regulation time ended in a one to one tie.

There were two overtime halves. The play was equal and no goals were scored. Both teams were exhausted.

The gold medal would be decided by shoot-out.

Coach Ron picked his shooters. "Luca, Farid, Trent, Reo and Chris — in that order."

No, it can't be, thought Chris. *I'm not a goal scorer. Amare is. I've never even taken a penalty kick in a real game.* His hands were shaking. *But I need to be confident. If I don't believe I can score, I probably won't.*

North Mississauga went first. The kicker blasted his shot into the left corner.

Luca scanned the net. Chris saw that the goalie was standing tall. *So Luca will shoot low,* he thought. Luca blasted the ball into the low right corner.

The second North Mississauga shooter caught Ben going the wrong way. The ball zipped into the wide-open side.

Farid lined up. He took four steps and fired. The ball shot right and the goalie moved towards it. The ball then spun into the top left corner. Farid had bent his penalty kick and had tricked the keeper.

The third North Mississauga shooter blasted one in.

Trent stepped back, ran in and pounded a low shot. *He didn't hide which way he was shooting,* thought Chris. It didn't matter. The kick was so powerful it ripped through the goalie's hands into the net.

The Final

The fourth Mississauga shooter aimed high right. Ben ran and leaped and got a hand on the ball. It broke through his fingers and into the net. *So close*, thought Chris.

Reo's shot wasn't hard, but it was accurate. He placed it beside the left post into the net.

The fifth Mississauga shooter shot low. Ben read the shooter and was in motion as the shooter's foot hit the ball. Ben dove headfirst and punched the ball out safely. Northern Mississauga had missed its last shot. Chris could win the game with a goal.

Chris placed the ball down. He took five steps back. *I can do this*, he told himself. *The keeper is crouched low, so I should shoot high. And he's closer to my left, trying to get me to shoot right. So I'll fake right and bend the ball left.* It was a risky move for Chris. Risky because he had just learned to curve the ball. Risky because he didn't have a lot of distance to work with. *But it feels right*, Chris thought. *I'm ready.*

Chris took five steps and hit the ball on the sweet spot. The ball fired right. The keeper ran in that direction and dove. The ball began to curve left, getting past the keeper and whizzing into the top left corner so hard it thrust the netting back.

Chris had scored the gold-medal-winning goal!

His teammates swarmed him. He fell to the ground and everyone piled on. There were tears in his eyes. He didn't wipe these tears away. They were tears of happiness. He was buried under a whole team of soccer players, but he felt lighter than he had in a long time.

The medals were awarded right there on the field.

"Hey, Chris, there goes your football field goal career," joked Trent.

"Yeah, good riddance, eh?" said Chris.

"Do you think you can come back to the Shamrocks next season?" asked Trent. "We sure could use you."

"I just might. I think I'm ready," said Chris. He thought about how far he had come. With a sport to play and a team behind him, he believed he could keep the depression from taking over, at least most of the time. "And I'll definitely be back with the Hotspurs. We've got to help Coach Dave win a championship, don't we!"

NOTE FOR READERS

If you think you have depression or any other mental health issue, or know someone else who does, help is not far away. Please talk to your parents, doctor or a school counsellor. If you are between the ages of five and twenty, you can call the Kids Help Phone at 1-800-668-6868. This 24/7 service is free, anonymous and confidential. It is also available by text (686868) or online via live chat (kidshelpphone.ca). The service provides professional counselling, information and referrals to help kids deal with mental health issues, addictions and well-being.

ACKNOWLEDGEMENTS

As always, I would like to thank Kat Mototsune, my editor, for her perceptive feedback and gracious support. She is a pleasure to work with and improves my work immeasurably.

The first readers of *The Comeback* were my kids, Michael and Grace. They provided many helpful suggestions and helped ensure I described the game of soccer as accurately as possible.

I would also like to thank Carrie Gleason for guiding the publication of my work, and William Brown for his assistance in promoting this book as well as my last, *The Playmaker*.

And finally, I'd like to thank all the librarians, teachers and booksellers who have placed my books in their libraries, schools and stores, and who work so hard to promote reading and literacy. You are very much appreciated.